Pump Two

J. Cherry

Content Warnings

This novella is not intended for anyone under the age of eighteen.

This novella features graphic sexual activities between two consenting adults and should in no way be used educationally, as an informational guide or to suggest how sex should be explored. These scenes are also not intended to represent realistic expectations of sexual activities.

Sexual activities featured in this book:
Breath play
Oral sex
Spit play
Public play/exhibitionism
Ass play
Object insertion

Playlist

Clairvoyant - MISOGI
Kill or Be Killed - Dirty Sweet
telepatía - Kali Uchis
Move for me - DXXDLY
METAMORPHOSIS - Sped Up - INTERWORLD -
Nightexpress - Kim
Pyramid - ALYSS
New Person, Same Old Mistakes - Tame Impala
Where You Belong - Little Dragon
Morning After Dark (Ft Nelly Furtado & SoShy) -
Timbaland
California Heaven - Medasin Remix - JAHKOY
SAOKO - ROSALÍA
Bother Me - CHUNG HA

For those who like smut and masked men.

Chapter 1
Violet

I've always hated the smell of gasoline. I think it's the fumes that drift up your nostrils and linger there for hours, leaving behind a stain that's almost impossible to remove.

Another thing I hate is customer-facing jobs. The whole thing about the customer *always* being right never sits well with me, especially when most of the time, they're definitely not.

It's almost comical how the two things I despise have now become significant aspects of my new job at a gas station.

I listen to my friend, Freya, mindlessly ramble about some story whilst painting her nails. Her upper body is casually perched next to the cash register as if working here is a last priority.

"Honestly, I used to sleep on the graveyard shift because it was so quiet. Nobody checks the cameras in here unless some crazy shit happens, like when we got robbed last year," she says indifferently, pointing gun fingers at me for emphasis. "So feel free to go on your phone or whatever."

Freya blows briefly on her left hand and moves on to paint her right. With her fast rambles, I can only manage to nod my head in response. I'm actually a little envious of her ability to switch off her surroundings whilst focusing on telling whatever story comes to mind.

"And how often does this gas station get robbed?" I ask, grabbing a gummy bear out of the packet that's sitting between us.

"It was only that one time and not a regular occurrence, I promise. If you get into any trouble, just call these numbers." She points to a list of emergency contacts taped to the counter. Her number stands out amongst the rest, encircled with hearts and doodles. Freya, as always, is completely unfazed by something as panic-inducing as a robbery.

We met a few years ago at a high school party. It was the first and last party of that nature I ever attended after discovering my then-boyfriend cheating on me. Two good things came out of that experience: I realized my ex was a scumbag and I met Freya.

She and I recently reconnected after bumping into each other during my hellish shift at the local grocery store. Like me, she was one of the few who didn't attend college after school.

"I'm *so* happy you want this job." She stops momentarily to lift her head and offers me a sweet smile before returning to her nails. "Since Davy left, I've been stuck working here all night. Considering my uncle co-owns this place, you'd think he would listen to my suggestions about hiring more workers. Yay to being understaffed," Freya exclaims sarcastically with false cheer.

Her family has worked at this gas station for years because it's owned half by her uncle and half by Mr. Simmons who bought it in the eighties or something.

"Did you not see the customer I was dealing with when you saw me working at the store? I was one more bad day away from quitting on the spot," I point out. "You literally saved me by offering me this job." Freya gives me a satisfied smirk, her eyes brightening at my words.

As I fiddle with some lighters on the counter, she continues to silently paint her nails. I take in the outdated gas station; it's so old that you can't even pay at the pump.

Grimacing, I study the yellowing walls and gray linoleum flooring, both of which were probably once a bright white. Only the cash register and coffee machine appear to have retained some semblance of modernity. The interior and exterior have definitely seen better days, and generations of locals must have borne witness to the aging over time.

Walking around the counter, I rub my foot on the worn-down spot in front of it. I look up when a customer slams down a six-pack of beers next to me with a resounding thud.

"Hey Frank, how can I help?" Freya addresses. She seems familiar with him and engages in casual banter whilst tentatively pressing the buttons on the cash register to avoid ruining her nails. We watch Frank pay and leave before Freya speaks again, "You know how to use the register, right? People constantly ask if we have any five dollars or ten dollars to exchange for bigger bills. Don't act like a bank and swap them or you'll run out of those fives and tens *fast*."

"Got it," I reply absentmindedly, flicking a lighter and watching the flame dance.

Freya closes her nail polish and places it under the counter, pausing to stare at my hair. With her easily distracted mind, she derails the conversation about the training at hand.

"God, I wish I didn't go so bold for my haircut. Why did I go from blonde to ginger and chop it to my shoulders? I must've been having a bad week." Freya assesses a strand of her hair with a look of disgust.

"Oh, come on! It's copper and it looks gorgeous," I respond truthfully. It really does look nice. A lot different from when we were in high school.

"It looks like ass, Vi," Freya sighs. "You've always had amazing style though, so I'll trust your opinion. Do you make clothes by the way? I'm loving this." Her gaze shifts from my hair to my outfit, and she reaches out to touch the fabric of my cardigan.

"Nope, I just draw and paint. Same old, same old," I reply.

I'm obsessed with my art, and I'm restraining myself from talking Freya's ear off about it at the brief mention of the topic.

"Oh yeah! I remember you telling me about that mural next to the market, it looks so good!" That mural took me ages; days of painting in the Arizona sun left me with the most painful sunburn ever, just the memory of it makes me cringe.

"Oh my god, I spent weeks on it. I wish I could get more commissions for public art because I'm already considering doing art or nothing. Unemployment, here I come," I joke. Obviously, I will be working until I reach full-time artist status. I kind of hope that speaking about how much I want it will somehow manifest it into happening…the artist stuff, not unemployment. Freya starts violently shaking her head at my words.

"I don't know if I'll be able to handle subbing in for this graveyard shift again. If you leave this job, I might just end up becoming unemployed with you, Vi." We both laugh and Freya offers me the last gummy bear. I decline and she eats it, throwing the packet in the trash. "But seriously, the station could do with a creative touch. It's so fucking ugly. I'll ask my uncle if you can add some color, then you can paint during your shift," Freya says whilst chewing, motioning to an empty wall next to some shelves.

She's right. I noticed the walls earlier, they're completely barren. I doubt that a fresh coat of paint has been within ten feet of the station since it was built.

"Yeah, that'd be amazing. I've been trying to build up my portfolio, but my art just isn't selling. Sometimes I wonder if I should have just gone to college. Maybe it would've helped jumpstart my career."

"Seriously, me too. Especially after my very brief stint in you-know-what. It feels like everyone is way ahead of me." Freya raises her brows and blows on her nails.

Whilst I haven't asked, I know that Freya partied and drank a fair bit during her senior year. It resulted in her spending a short time after graduation in some alcohol or drug rehabilitation scheme. She's adamant that her parents overreacted, but I don't know the whole story.

"We can still go to college, there's no age limit."

"Yeah, but my main motivation right now is the fear of missing out. All of my friends are at college. Will, Helena..." She continues listing off a handful of people from school whose names I've heard but aren't super familiar with. "At least you're here. I don't know if the partying there would be worth the questioning from my parents. I'm trying to slowly edge back into the social scene here and it's scary. The drinking was honestly not bad, but I don't want to fall down that hole with my mom again." Seeing Freya anxious is a rare sight, the topic is obviously bothering her.

"Well, don't feel like you're alone in this. I also need to get out more, and I don't drink that much. Maybe we could hang out together?" I suggest. I feel like spending more time with Freya could benefit both of us.

"Really? I know I'm too old to care about what my family thinks. They're just so crazy and—" Freya cuts herself off, her eyes sad. "Anyways, that'd be nice, Vi." A hint of pink tinges her high cheekbones, as if she's a little embarrassed for showing a vulnerable side of herself.

Our conversation is interrupted by another customer, and Freya lets me take the wheel. She watches me serve a few people before wrapping up the brief, informal training.

"Easy, right? Like, no customers come at night and you have this bad boy." Freya leans over the counter and slaps the plastic divider that separates me from the customers, making it wobble slightly. She yanks her hand back, remembering that she's just painted her nails. "Make sure everything's stocked and cleaned for the morning shift and you're good to go. Sounds okay?" Freya presses on a nail to check if it's dried and looks up from her hand to me, waiting for a response.

"Sounds great, I'll keep you updated with my first shift." I think my tone sounds a little bored because Freya looks at me amused, as if she knows exactly how I feel.

"Please do! I'm going to head to the gym now. You know...trying to get in shape for summer." Freya slaps her torso, the skin of which is visible in her matching cropped tee and leggings set. She then flexes her bicep, causing me to let out a sharp laugh.

"Have fun, Freya," I say with a smile as the lingering scent of her nail polish wafts around where I'm standing.

"Later, Vi!" Freya beams at me and exits the building. I watch her walk toward her car through the window, music blasting as she leaves the parking lot.

The station is now cloaked by an eerie silence in the absence of her enthusiastic personality.

I tap my fingers on the counter and look around the cash register. There's a box of lost property, and some magazines take residence on a shelf underneath. The magazines are ancient. They even have celebrities on the covers that I completely forgot existed. I'm convinced that the cash register hasn't been tidied since before I was born.

On the shelf behind me, there's a radio that I switch to some rock station. The music actually gives the place some life. *What did Freya do to keep herself entertained here?* My footsteps tap against the floor as I meander down the aisles, dragging my finger along the top of some shelves which show evidence of dust—lots of it. I guess I might as well find something to do if there are no customers.

I locate the utility closet, pulling the dangling string in the doorway to turn on the light so that I can find a cloth. It doesn't turn on. I pull the string again…nothing. With one hard yank, the string comes loose, and the closet remains pitch black. *Great, that's probably coming out of my paycheck.*

I decide to make do with what I have and prop the door open, allowing the light from the station to illuminate the closet.

Dusting turns out to be more therapeutic than I expected because when the bell rings to signal that someone has entered the store, I'm reminded that I have customers to serve. I almost jump for joy at the sign of life and move to the register, spotting a group of teenagers walking around.

The smell of marijuana trails after them, and I give them a small smile as they disappear down an aisle. I keep an eye on them through the CCTV behind the counter. Watching them reminds me of some of the kids I went to school with.

At school, I would tuck myself inside the art classroom whenever I didn't have class. I'd see classmates sneak behind the building to smoke a joint, amongst other things. Whilst I was by no means a loner, I wish I didn't play it so safe in high school.

Like most of my peers, I was a good student and avoided trouble like my life depended on it. I was scared of getting told off, got with the guy with good prospects, and followed the rules.

It was as simple as that and despite doing everything by the book, my life was so boring. Now it's three years later and almost *nothing* has changed. The only thing that's different is that I'm now single.

I'm drawn out of my thoughts when the group of teenagers pile a bunch of chips in front of me. They must set the tone for the type of customers I get for the rest of the night because from that point on, it's either high teenagers or older men who come in to buy gas, alcohol, cigarettes, and even those e-cigarette things.

I'm redrawing a price sign, and my ears perk up when I hear a loud rumbling. Curiosity gets the better of me, so I peer out of the window to see a sleek, black motorcycle pulling into the gas station lot.

The rider doesn't remove their helmet, which means that I can't make out a face. I can, however, tell that they're well-built despite the thick black leather that encases their body.

When I think of motorcycles, my mind conjures the image of bearded older men who smoke cigars and are more rugged. This person seems to be the opposite of my preconception.

The biker makes their way to the entrance, and I resume my drawing position as his large, gloved hand opens the gas station door. The bell rings loudly, and the pungent smell of gasoline seeps into the station. I swallow sharply as the intimidating figure gets bigger with each step they take toward me.

This person is huge. *Fuck.*

I shrink back a little when large boots come to a thumping stop opposite me. The helmet actually looks really cool, and despite having a better view of them, it gives no indication of what their face looks like. It's almost like it's made of a one-sided, see-through material. The biker can obviously see me, but I can't see them.

The angle of their head tells me they're looking at the half-drawn sign on the counter. I can't shake the feeling that they're sizing me up too.

"Hey," I squeak out and clear my throat. I try to make what I think is eye contact with them, only to end up looking directly into my own reflection.

"Twenty on pump two." His voice is so deep, it's like a baritone lull.

"Sure." I input numbers into the cash register, having to void and re-input because of my fumbling hands. "Do you need anything else today? Perhaps a coffee?" I'm trying to force a conversation just so I can hear Biker Guy's voice again. I've never heard someone speak with a voice that deep before. He doesn't reply. I smile at him politely, only to once again look at my reflection. I notice a stray hair and discretely use his helmet like a mirror, tucking the strand behind my ear.

It's awkward speaking to a faceless man, and his tedious responses make things more uncomfortable.

"No, thank you. Maybe next time," he says, pulling out his card.

Next time? I nod and gesture at the card in his gloved hand.

"Whenever you're ready," I say.

He suddenly tucks the card back into his pocket and pulls out a fifty-dollar bill, placing it on the counter.

"Do you have anything smaller?" I ask, nervous about accepting something so large. He's going to run me out of change, and Freya's words about acting like a bank come to mind.

"Keep the change." *What?*

"But—" I don't have time to finish my sentence because he's already leaving. My heart beats erratically in my chest like a wild creature demanding release, its rhythm persisting until the loud bike engine is nothing but a murmur down the road.

Chapter 2
Violet

For the next week, my shifts go by smoothly. Aside from the odd seedy comment from creepy guys and rowdy drunks, the job itself is laid back, and it gives me time to draw.

Freya's uncle has given me permission to create artwork on the gas station walls. Unfortunately, my creative streak can only focus on drawing one thing: a self-portrait of myself in the reflection of a biker's helmet. The same biker that I served last week. Dramatic, I know.

He had casually mentioned buying a coffee the next time he visited, and I am still clinging to those words as if they're a sacred promise.

My peace is disrupted by the bell, which rings when an

angry-looking man who just paid for gas marches back into the store. I quickly put my sketchbook away and watch as the customer slams his meaty hands on the counter. My eyes trail up his hairy arms, landing on his face that's wrinkled in disdain.

This is not going to be good.

"Your pump's fucking broken! You trying to scam me or something, girl?" His voice raises, and I feel my body begin to fill with panic. Being shouted at is one of the worst feelings.

"The pump is broken?" I ask weakly, slowly placing my pencil on the counter.

"Didn't you hear me the first time, sweetheart?" The nickname should be comforting, yet it has the opposite effect when laced with the hostility in this man's tone.

"I can come and have a look, or you can go to a different pump. You paid in cash, so I can refund you if you would like?" I suggest, silently hoping that he'll opt for the refund.

"I want to use the pump I'm parked at. I'm not moving my truck until it's working!" he yells, leaning forward and pointing his finger at where his truck sits idly next to the pump. Is this really the hill this guy wants to die on?

I suck in a deep breath and idiotically step around the counter. I'm not one for confrontation, but in this situation, I'd rather just try to solve the issue and get this asshole to leave. His gaze drops to my outfit, and he rolls his eyes.

"Fucking women," he mumbles.

14

I'm literally wearing a crop top and low-rise jeans. I itch to make a comment about me being the closest he's ever been to a woman and instead, choose to ignore his words to go outside and look at the pump. When I test it, it's obviously broken because the handle is stuck. Still, no reason for this guy to be mad, though. It's hardly the end of the world.

"I can try to call for help, but it's three a.m., and I don't know how long it'll take for someone to come out. I highly suggest using one of our *many* other pumps," I explain, my tone laced with artificial kindness.

He steps closer, no doubt to intimidate me. It's obvious that he dislikes my answer and will probably continue to refuse any of the well-working pumps around us.

"I don't want to use the *other pumps*," he hisses, specs of saliva flying under the gas station lights. Blood is roaring in my ears, and I feel a little uneasy now that it's just me with this increasingly aggressive guy in the middle of an empty gas station.

The nearest place is a closed mechanic store about a mile down the road. With no sign of nearby help, I stand my ground as I feel myself gradually losing patience with the customer's stubborn, misogynistic attitude.

"Well, you're going to have to," I grit back. *Go me.*

We go back and forth for a while until I hear a distant roar of a motorcycle. I silently pray that it's the hot biker from last week showing up to conveniently come and save me from this unwinnable battle that I'm having. I've been constantly snapping my head to look out of the gas station window whenever a bike passes—a humble reminder that I need to get a grip.

"You're fucking useless!" the angry guy shouts, yanking me out of my thoughts. His shining, bald head turns red, and he looks almost cartoonish. I expect steam to start blowing from his ears any second now.

He continues to back me up across the parking lot until I'm nearly in front of the gas station door. I refuse to react to his words and feed into his disrespect, so I stay silent.

This makes him furious.

He storms toward me, and I step back. I keep stepping back until my heel knocks against the ground, causing me to lose my footing and topple backward.

The loud, high-pitch sound of tires screeching echoes through the station lot, just as my backside hits the ground. My breath is knocked out of my lungs, and I squeeze my eyes shut upon impact.

I take a few seconds to gather myself. When I open my eyes again, the angry guy is now standing over me. He's still rambling about the one pump he's set his heart on, his wretched voice continuing to invade my ears.

"Get away from her," a deep, recognizable voice sounds from behind him. I crane my neck and see a familiar leather figure. *Biker Guy.* I release a deep sigh of relief.

"You don't want to defend this cunt, man. She's fucking useless, can't even fix the pump I'm using." I flinch a little at the name I've just been called. *Cunt, seriously?*

Biker Guy tips his head to the side as if inspecting the man like an ant under a magnifying glass. His helmeted head looks slowly around the station.

"I can see several other pumps that work." The tone of his voice doesn't shift, but I can sense some anger.

"That's not the fucking point!" the customer spits.

"Use another pump or leave." Biker Guy steps closer to the man, his helmet making him look like some sort of Gotham-esque vigilante. The customer clenches his fists and starts walking away to his truck, turning to glare at me after a few steps.

"Dumb whore," he barks and spits on the ground in front of him.

He tries to use his shoulder to shove past the man I have now dubbed as 'Biker Guy', and a gloved hand reaches out, grabbing the customer's throat. Biker Guy brings his helmeted head so close to the angry man, that his scared, rapid breathing causes a small part of the helmet's front exterior to fog up.

"Call her a name other than the one on her name tag, and I will shove one of those gasoline pumps so far down your throat, you will bleed from the inside out," Biker Guy snarls. All initial calmness has completely evaporated from his being. "You'll never be able to look at a pump the same way again...or be physically capable of complaining about one."

Holy fuck.

In one hard shove, he propels the customer so far forward that the momentum causes him to slam against his truck. Biker Guy doesn't even watch the man drive off. Instead, he walks directly to me and crouches down to check my body for injuries. He uses a gloved finger to tap under my chin, forcing me to close my gawking mouth and look up at him.

"You good, Sweetness?" I nod in response, unbelieving that I might've actually manifested this. He helps me to my feet, and I inspect my hands which are cut up a little on the palms. "He hurt you?" Biker Guy says roughly whilst holding my wrists to inspect the grazes.

"The ground hurt me. I'm lucky the customer didn't lay a finger on me." I feel his lingering gaze on my body before he slowly guides me into the gas station.

With my stinging hands and bruised ass, I hobble alongside him until I'm behind the cash register. Quickly, I write an 'out of order' notice for the gas pump. I wince as the pen presses against my very minor injuries. Biker Guy places his hand over mine to stop me from writing. His gentle touches in the past few minutes make me realize that he has shown more tenderness toward me than my ex-boyfriend did in the entire year that we were together. The thought causes me to laugh softly. This seems to pique Biker Guy's curiosity and he tilts his head at me.

"Go clean up," he says firmly. I scurry away to the bathroom to do exactly that. When I return to the register, I see Biker Guy outside working on the pump. Not only has he saved me from a crazy customer, but he's also trying to fix the pump for me. *Who is this man?*

I tear my gaze away from him and search behind the counter for a first aid kit. As I use an alcohol wipe to clean my small cuts, I continue to watch him through the window. He still has his helmet on, which strikes me as odd. I can't imagine how impractical it must be. He faces my direction whilst he works, his head occasionally lifting up in my direction. I sit behind the counter as stiff as a board, trying not to react when his attention shifts to me.

"Fixed your pump," he says when he finally enters the store after messing with broken machinery. His words are sharp as if he's annoyed. Is he annoyed at *me*? I feel like I've inconvenienced him massively tonight. I fidget a little and clasp my hands together self-reassuringly.

"Thank you for your help and sorry about that customer. He was horrible. Thank god I only have three hours left." I laugh nervously. Biker Guy still doesn't take his helmet off, and I'm staring awkwardly at my reflection again. His hands clench, leather gloves fisted in what I can only assume is frustration. I stare at his helmet like my brain will just magically conjure the most accurate image of his face.

I'm so invested in this stranger that fawning over him almost feels dirty. The bar for men is clearly in hell because all it takes is a deep voice and basic human decency for me to form a crush.

"How can I help you today?" I ask, moving on from

checking him out.

"Ten dollars on pump two..." he pauses as if unsure and partially turns to face the aisles. "And coffee."

I nod slowly, confused about his hesitance.

"Sure, the machine is over there." I point to the self-fill hot drink machine. I know a lot of people come in for coffee, but for some reason, deep down in my gut, I wish he had come here to see me again. This gas station is out of the way, located on a barely used road that spans the distance between two neighboring towns. I almost refuse to believe that he could end up here a second time unless by choice.

He strolls over to the coffee station like he has nothing better to do with his time and fills up the cheap, cardboard cup before walking back to pay.

"Eleven-fifty, please. For the gas and drink." He pulls out a twenty. "Oh, and I'm not keeping the change this time," I say in a light joke to ease the tension between us.

"Keep the change, Sweetness." He's called me that nickname again, and my stomach swarms with warmth. Definitely not mad at me. If he was, he wouldn't have called me that, right? Unless I'm severely misjudging my social interactions.

"No—"

"I'll make you keep the change whether you like it or not." He makes a show of looking at my name tag by placing his hands on the counter and leaning forward. "Violet."

"I'd like to see you try," I respond, trying hard not to show

20

any reaction to the way he says my name.

Are we arguing or flirting? Whatever it is, I like it.

Love it, actually.

I place the money on the counter and push it toward him. He grabs it and I step back, relieved that he's willingly taken it. Then, he's moving. Not to exit the station…but toward me.

Deliberate slowness guides his steps as he encircles the counter, his presence warming my back. I'm rendered motionless, seizing up when he shoves the money into my back pocket. I release a gasp as my already low jeans are pushed even further down. Then, just as fast as he came behind the counter, he's back in front of it. The nerve of this guy! I can't tell if he's brooding, flirty, or just completely unhinged.

All I know is that I'm furiously turned on and surprisingly unafraid.

"I didn't think you'd actually do it!" I exclaim. Biker Guy lets out a laugh so deep, my body vibrates at the tone.

"I hate turning down challenges."

"You're not meant to come behind the counter. This is for my safety to protect *me* from customers like *you*," I lecture, tapping my nail against the plastic separation screen.

"Okay, I promise I won't come behind the counter again. Sorry for breaking your little rule, Violet," he drawls.

"It's a big rule and no, I wasn't challenging you. I was just…" I don't have an explanation because I *know* I was somewhat challenging him. I just didn't think he'd follow through.

"I'm not one for following rules, but I'll keep that in mind for next time if it keeps you satisfied." Once again, he mentions a next time.

Just like that, the butterflies in my stomach have gone from a gentle flutter to a frantic beating of wings. The words I'm supposed to reply with don't come, and I opt for nibbling at my bottom lip instead. For some odd and unknown reason, I'm attracted to everything about this guy; from his voice and helmet to the way he says certain words. I haven't even seen his face yet.

"Oh, and thanks for keeping the change," he says.

With that, he flicks up the visor on his helmet. Impenetrable green eyes look back at me. They're framed with moderately thick, brown eyebrows, and the skin around them doesn't look aged. I'd probably put him in his mid to late twenties. *Thank god.*

There's a flicker of amusement in his gaze before he turns. I stare at his back as he walks out of the door, leaving his coffee behind. I continue to watch him fill up his bike until he rides off into the night, giving me a small salute through the window when he departs.

My back pocket burns my skin at the memory of his hand, my insides screaming and yearning for this man I don't even know. It's not a lot, but I know sex appeal when I see it—or in this case, feel it and hear it. Maybe it's the biker getup with the leather jacket. Either way, I feel a bit out of sorts.

I immediately take out my sketchbook and start drawing his eyes out of fear that I'll forget them. I sketch for the rest of my shift, trying to get his features as accurate as possible. It's only when I clock out a few hours later that I'm convinced I can hear the low hum of a motorbike for my entire journey home.

Chapter 3
Biker Guy

I'm impatient. It's by far my worst trait. In the past two weeks, I find my patience being tested when it comes to a certain gas station cashier.

Through no fault of her own, I want Violet, and I'm trying to hold back in fear that I'll scare her away. So far, I'm failing.

This is by no means a love-at-first-sight situation, but lust on the other hand? Maybe.

It's been four days since I last visited her, and I plan on going to the gas station tonight.

The first time I saw her was when I foolishly decided not to fill up before going on a ride at night. I almost ended up running out of gas, no thanks to my lack of organization. Violet's gas station was the closest one that appeared on my phone's navigation app, which showed that it was open overnight. When I arrived, I was met with a pair of dark eyes that were curiously peeking out of the window.

For someone who seemed shy at first, the way she shows her emotions is loud—her confidence seemingly amplified by my faceless appearance.

Our last meeting didn't start with pleasantries because I was too busy seeing red. Some customer was giving Violet shit, and I arrived just in time to get him to fuck off. I would've handled it a lot more violently if I wasn't so eager to make sure that she was okay. By the time I left, her shy demeanor and obvious attraction to me became completely addicting, and now, I just want to go back to see how much I can tease her.

I'm almost tempted to ride more often so I can deplete my gas and use it as an excuse to go back to the station. I can't believe I'm considering increasing the size of my ecological footprint just to have a reason to visit her.

Her reaction when I lifted my visor was hilarious. I didn't know it was possible for my eyes to elicit such a response from Violet. With her puffy lips opened wide in a silent gasp, it took everything in me not to meet them with my own.

I could stare at her face all day; angular and strong, adorned with full lips and sharp eyes. Black hair cascades over her shoulders, and under the fluorescent lights of the gas station, it has a sheen that makes it look like silk. In her nervous rambling, she let it slip what time her graveyard shift ended. After that fucker gave her trouble yesterday, I rode around for a bit and then followed her to make sure she got home safe.

"Bro."

I shake my head as if coming out of a trance, my hair coming slightly loose from its hair tie. My best friend jerks his chin at me. "Choose your character," Kas says. I forgot we were playing a fighting game on his console, so I mindlessly do as I'm told.

"I don't know why I'm playing with you. I haven't won once," I complain, sinking back into the couch.

"We're good at different things," he replies nonchalantly, and I throw him a look of annoyance as I start moving my character around. I manage to land a couple of punches that don't seem to do anything against Kas' character.

"Yeah, and you're good at everything," I tell him, chaotically smashing the buttons on my controller as he casually works a combination to beat the living shit out of my on-screen fighter. "How long will it take until you beat me this time? Ten seconds? Five?" I question, leaning forward to get a better look at the screen and watch Kas' hit streak increase as he gets closer to winning.

"Eh, I'll give it a minute." We go head-to-head, my controller vibrating with each punch he lands on me for the next sixty seconds. The screen promptly flashes with my defeat, and I throw the controller to my side.

"Unfair," I mutter. "There's no way it's possible to beat someone that fast. I hope one day someone kicks your ass on this game."

"The day someone beats me will be the day I get knocked out in the ring." I huff out a laugh and he grins at me.

Kas is an amateur MMA fighter, and he is unbeatable. Both of us earn our money from sports; whilst he's in the ring, I'm out racing bikes.

In my father's lack of presence following my parents' divorce when I was much younger, he bought me various vehicles to make up for his absence. I spent my time fixing them up and riding them for fun. It went from a hobby into a career, and I now find myself doing both for quick cash.

I stand up and stretch, yawning at a volume that's unnecessarily loud. I'm starting to feel the aftermath of my insomnia that plagues me most nights.

"I'm going to bed," I announce to Kas who looks at me skeptically.

"I hear you leave every night to go on a ride," he says. Kas speaks mostly in statements—a quiet observer. He's aware of every single little movement around him, and it's what also makes him so good at his sport. He's blunt and whilst seemingly silent, his actions speak louder than words.

This is definitely the case when he uses his fists.

"Since your nosey ass is so interested, I can't sleep and riding helps." He nods, watching me with suspicion as I start to walk out of the room.

"Oh, by the way, Micah is hosting a post-fight party after my fight next month," Kas calls from behind me, just as I begin to round the corner to the stairs. Micah is someone we used to hang out with for a while. We became close to him after he bailed me out of jail a few years ago for getting into a fight at one of his parties.

During high school and college, Micah was known for throwing some of the wildest parties in the region. I never attended them on a regular basis, but his house was the perfect venue for people to engage in less-than-holy activities. His parents were constantly involved in their dodgy businesses abroad, so they were either none the wiser, or just didn't care.

College-goers from multiple towns would attend his parties, and I'm convinced that some high schoolers managed to sneak in. Nowadays, Micah works as an event planner in Los Angeles and hosts some of the hottest celebrity events.

"Is this not below his pay grade? A party back in his hometown?" I question from the large archway that separates the lounge and hallway.

"Yeah, I don't know." I take Kas' lack of enthusiasm about the party as my cue to stop asking him questions and head upstairs to try and nap for a while.

My body, with no choice but to rest, manages to allow me a few hours of sleep before waking up at one in the morning.

With some sort of dormancy in the brain during my power

nap, I feel more reset and energetic than usual. I don't know if it's because I actually slept for a while, or because I'm going to see Violet. It's probably the latter because I feel like my crush on her is becoming a bit *obsessive*.

I quickly shower and when I step out to dry myself, the blast of cold air against my wet skin reminds me to wear my ski mask under my helmet to keep my face warm when I ride tonight. I pull on my usual jeans and tee, then slip on the ski mask. It feels more uncomfortable than usual. My hair has reached its longest length ever and now extends down to my shoulders. The sensation of it against the mask is beginning to make me itch.

Impulsively, I rip off the black fabric and search for an electric razor in the bathroom drawer, stripping off my clothes to avoid getting hair on them. After thirty minutes of standing butt naked and covered in hair trimmings, I've completely shaved off my hair—adopting a similar buzz cut to Kas.

With no time to waste, I quickly rinse off in the shower to rid myself of any stray hairs before seeing Violet. It takes me around an hour to travel to the gas station on my bike. I shut off the engine and position myself in the shadows of the building to light up a cigarette.

The parking lot is quiet, and I wonder if Violet gets the creeps here at night. The gas station window is almost as wide as the brick wall it's on, so you can see pretty much everything inside. From my position right now, I can see

29

Violet's long hair through the window as she...stands on a six-foot ladder.

Yeah, I don't think so.

I quickly stomp out my cigarette on the ground and walk inside. She's drawing something on the wall of the store. I can't see what she's working on and right now, I'm more bothered by her standing on the ladder.

"Do you know how dangerous it is to stand on a six-foot ladder alone with nobody within a mile to hear you if you fall?" She doesn't respond and carries on drawing.

"I'm fine, everything's under control," she says, finally acknowledging my arrival.

I grip the ladder and give it a light shake. Violet lets out a squeal and grips the top rung, glaring down at me in confused anger.

Despite my tendency to be quieter during our previous encounters, I can't help but find her reaction amusing. The last time I visited, my words were clipped in anger due to the asshole customer. I also pissed off Violet by overstepping a plastic barrier to give her change.

I admit, I was out of order to place the money in her pocket myself, but I don't regret it.

She continues to look down at me a little perplexed and descends the ladder to walk to the counter.

"How can I help?" she asks dryly, her brown eyes glistening with a combination of annoyance, curiosity, and something else I can't quite put my finger on. I lean against the old counter as if I have no other care in the world.

"Ten on pump two."

Her dark eyes linger on my helmet and after a few moments, she punches in the amount so I can pay. I leave to fill up my bike and instantly return to the station.

"Forgot to buy coffee," I say, pulling out my card. I pay and slowly walk to the coffee station.

"Are you going to drink it this time?" she calls, and I smile from behind my helmet.

"What's it to you?" I counter, her words reminding me that I didn't take my coffee with me last time. I genuinely forgot. Now I realize that to drink it, I'd have to remove my helmet and mask—based on Violet's reaction to my appearance, I'm reluctant to do exactly that.

"A waste of coffee."

"The coffee was for you," I lie. Admittedly, getting coffee buys me a bit of time because it means that I can stay longer in Violet's presence by dawdling at the coffee station. Now that I don't intend to drink it, my lie appears to flatter her.

"Well...thanks, I guess." She shuffles on her feet and presses her lips together, tucking some hair behind her ear.

After filling my coffee, I place the cup on the counter in front of her and move away to check out what she was drawing on the wall. I manage to make out the outline of a sandwich, and I can feel Violet's eyes on me as I begin to notice more and more drawings of food items on the wall.

"Are you okay?" she asks, eyeing me suspiciously when I

make my way back toward her. Only then do I realize how creepy I probably seem still hanging around the gas station.

"Nice drawing." I tilt my head at the wall.

"Thanks, I'm trying to improve the interior," she says, my eyes tracing the shape of her mouth as she speaks. We're looking at each other with mutual intensity. It feels as if we are both trying to smother our attraction to each other and failing to do so.

"You're talented," I say, leaning on the counter.

"You think?"

"Wouldn't say it if I didn't think so." She blushes a little and it only accentuates her already glowing face.

"Would you like a seat or something?" Violet laughs uncomfortably, watching me stand awkwardly in front of her.

"I'd love a seat, actually."

She looks at me as if she was expecting me to decline, her hands trembling a little when she grabs a spare chair from behind the cash register. I take it from her, and she pulls out a sketchbook. *Does this girl ever stop drawing?*

I sit on the chair, removing my gloves and jacket in the process. Violet clutches her sketchpad to her chest like an old woman would clutch her pearls. Her eyes scan all over my upper body, unsure of where to look.

"I'm taking off my jacket, not flashing you my dick. Relax," I mumble, hoping that my tone is more flirtatious than crude. Violet's eyes widen so much that if she's not careful, they might roll out of her head. I feel like I'm fucking this up.

Actually, I *know* I'm fucking this up.

Her mouth opens, and nothing more than a silent choke escapes her lips. She clears her throat and straightens her posture, ready to try again.

"You wouldn't show me your dick, you can't even show your face."

Damn, I didn't know she had it in her. I let out a low whistle of surprise. She suddenly starts drawing, her slender fingers wrapped unusually tight around the pencil. It's sweet that she's trying her best to keep her cool.

"Is that another challenge? Remember what happened last time?" I tip my head toward the counter.

"I'm not wrong, though," she says, a light flush painting her face.

"You underestimate me. Hiding my face is foreplay, but we can skip that if you'd rather?"

I lean back and spread my legs wider, my hands resting on top of my belt buckle. She does a double take and opens her mouth in shock, quickly shielding her eyes with her sketchpad. "I'm playing, Violet. I'm just trying to break the ice."

She peeks over her pad as if to check if I've exposed myself. Then, she exaggeratedly sighs in either relief or disappointment when she sees my bottom half covered—as to which one it is, I can't tell.

"You're very forward. Are you flirting or teasing?" she

asks, her lips twitching as if she's trying to restrain a smile.

"Both, I think you're cute."

"Cute?"

Cute, beautiful, stunning, angelic. The only thing on my mind for the past week. Yeah, cute. *Sure.*

"Yes, of course I think you're cute. I'm not blind." She purses her lips in thought at my answer.

"You're a bit too forward." Definitely not the response I was expecting. I would be a little offended if I was trying to take it slow, but as always, I'm impatient. I ignore her and focus on what she's doing.

"Is that a car?" I ask, and she turns her drawing pad to face me.

"Yeah, I saw it outside earlier," she says, dragging her eyes away from me. It's one of the most amazing sketches I've ever seen in my life.

"From memory?" I lean further over the counter to get a better look at the page. The plastic divider stops me and from this angle, I can only just tell that she's wearing those flared jeans from the other day. A sliver of skin peeks above the low waist, and I force my eyes away.

"Yep." She pops the 'P' like it's just normal to draw an entire classic car accurately from memory. I'm so impressed that I don't even know what to say, so I just sit back down and watch her draw. It's therapeutic as fuck.

She turns over to a fresh page and begins sketching something new. Her eyes dart between me and the paper as we enjoy a comfortable silence for a while.

"I need you to take the helmet off so I can draw your face." She circles her pencil in the air to emphasize her words.

Absolutely not.

"Just draw me with the helmet on."

"You sound muffled all the time, and it looks like you'd get hot under there. Usually, bikers take it off." Yeah, it is a bit stuffy under here, though a little more comfortable thanks to my freshly shaved head. And yes, I would take it off. But since she is unable to see my face, it adds a little fun to our interactions. It encourages her to come out of her shell.

"No, you like the mask." She pauses for a second and then carries on drawing. Her body language speaks for her when she doesn't—I know she likes not seeing my face.

"So? You get to know where I work, my name, and my face." She sketches more aggressively whilst glaring at me. "Can I at least know your name?"

"If I tell you, I die."

"Oh, shut up." Violet pouts in a way that fails to smother a smile, her eyes trailing over my thighs as she sketches. Her memory of the car she sketched was pretty good, and I'm sure she doesn't need to look at me so much. I'm not going to complain because I love the feeling of her eyes on me.

We don't talk whilst she sketches, and around fifteen minutes later, she's done.

"Alright, here it is," she announces.

She rips the paper out of the sketchbook, and I notice

doodles on the back. Violet hands me the paper face down. Upon closer inspection, it looks like she's been practicing her signature on this sheet because different versions of her name merge into various Violet flowers all over one side of the sketch.

I flip the page over to see the drawing that she's just done. The sketch is definitely me. But there's one detail that is completely inaccurate: My head. Violet has drawn a clown mask instead of my helmet.

I don't react, folding up the paper and placing it in my pocket. I cross my arms over my chest and look around the store, pretending to act indifferent as I try to fight back a smile. Giggles bubble up from Violet's throat, the sound causing a jolt of heat to rush through me.

"That commission will be two-hundred dollars." She holds her hand out and purses her lips. I know she's messing around, but I reach into my back pocket and take out my wallet. "Kidding," she says quickly.

Honestly, I'd pay her and she knows that. She could probably empty me of every penny I have and I'd say thank you.

"Look at you, cracking jokes. You're lucky that you're on the other side of that counter after that drawing," I say in a mock threat, and she rolls her eyes.

"Well, I need to go and wash my hands." She holds up her palms and twists her wrists to show me smudges of graphite on them, her bracelets jingling with the movement.

I watch her like a predator watching its prey as she slowly rounds the counter. I lean forward ready to pounce. She looks at me with a small, challenging smile before darting forward. She doesn't get very far because I stand up fast and loop my arm around her waist, pulling her back against my body.

"Nice try, Sweetness," I whisper. My lips graze her earlobe, and her hair is fragrant with something sweet and earthy. She freezes, the heat of her stomach radiating against my forearm.

The sound of the bell is the only thing that gets me to pull away from her. I drag my hand lightly over her midriff as I unlatch myself from her body, squeezing her waist before letting go. Her body goes unnaturally taut, and she walks stiffly to the cash register.

When the customer finally departs, she darts into the small bathroom at the back of the store. I can hear the faint sound of running water before she emerges a minute later. Her hands are wet and glistening as she shakes them in front of her to dry them off.

"Why did you come here today?" she asks, walking behind the counter and grabbing some napkins to finish drying her hands with. Good question. Why did I come here?

"To see you," I reply honestly.

"To see me? Seriously?" I nod and she looks unbelieving of my answer. "Seems like a waste of gas if you ask me. We're in the middle of nowhere, so it probably costs you an entire tank just to come here," she says, brushing off the fact that I came here to see her specifically.

"Oh, thank god you work at a gas station." I feign relief, and she forcefully slides a pencil across the counter at me with the obvious intention of hitting me with it. I catch it deftly in my palm, twirling it between my fingers. I can feel her watching my hand as I play with it.

"Did you come here to check up on me after last time?" Violet asks, her voice laced with amusement.

"No, I knew you were okay," I grin.

"You followed me home." Her words take on a questioning lilt. I can tell that she already knows the answer.

"Maybe."

"I heard your bike," she says, confirming my suspicion. "You wanted me to know that you were following me."

"Maybe you imagined it because you wanted me to follow you home or something," I tease. Violet flushes a little, which tells me that I'm not entirely wrong.

"You're stalking me," she accuses, her lips curving upwards. She's completely unconcerned. Her reaction is relieving for me, but her willingness to trust me is somewhat alarming. Is she this trusting toward everyone?

"That's a bold statement, at least pretend to be scared." Violet's smile grows, and she covers her mouth with a lightly tanned hand to stifle a laugh.

"I'm sorry, I can't take you seriously with your helmet on. It reminds me of the Power Rangers." I grip the pencil she launched at me earlier and pretend to stab myself in the heart with it in response to her jest. She smiles and rolls her eyes, fiddling with a piece of her hair.

That sentence alone has me wanting to rip off the black plastic encasing my head. She seems oddly unfazed about me following her home, even if she can't take me seriously. I don't know if it's because she genuinely thinks I'm unserious and doesn't care, or because she feels safe around me.

"So, if you're not showing your face, can you tell me about yourself, Biker Guy?"

"Biker Guy? Creative. You couldn't come up with something cooler?" Violet lets out a small huff.

"Sorry, Mr. Pump Two. Your fault for not giving me your name and being too scared to take off your helmet. Makes it hard when I'm looking at my reflection every time we talk." I ignore her terrible nickname and decide to let her in on why I'm hesitant to reveal my face.

"This is what makes it fun. You have to admit, you would find it boring if you knew everything about me, including my face."

"Yeah, I guess it's…entertaining," she says, her eyes lingering on my body for what may be the hundredth time tonight. "When are you coming here again?"

"I'll keep you anticipating my next arrival, Violet." I'm being annoying on purpose, and she knows because she side-eyes me whilst reaching under the counter for something.

"I preferred it when you were broody and angry," she grumbles. I can't tell if she's joking because funnily enough,

I'm actually enjoying today's conversation. I guess talking to Violet when I'm not seconds away from chasing after a customer that disrespects her and beating him senseless will make anything enjoyable. "Wanna play?" She places a deck of cards on the counter.

It's like every time we talk, we find something that will prolong our time in each other's company. I like that she's getting more comfortable with me, whether it's because of my helmet, our natural chemistry, or a combination of both.

"Sure, I'll shuffle." I scoot my chair forward and for the next thirty minutes, we play until I finally decide to go home. When I make it to my bed, I manage to get a full eight hours of rest for the first time in a while.

I don't want to point fingers, but I think I know the reason why.

Chapter 4
Violet

He's here, again. It's been five days—five *painfully* long days since I last saw him. The low rumbling of his bike shoots straight through me as soon as he enters the lot. I'm tempted to go to the window so I can get a closer look at him.

He swings his leg off his bike and pushes the kickstand down with his boot, retreating into the darkness of the parking lot. Like last time, he reappears a few minutes later. Upon entering the gas station, the smell of cigarettes follows him, and I try not to scrunch my nose in displeasure.

"You really can't stay away from me," I say over the sound of the bell.

"Someone's confident today." He flips up his visor so I can see his playful, green eyes.

"I think you're the one that's confident here." I twist up my hair and clip it back with a large claw clip to keep my hands busy.

"I'm always confident," he says as he removes his leather gloves and shrugs off his jacket to reveal a black tee that hugs muscular arms. I almost collapse right where I stand behind the cash register, again.

Where am I meant to look? Do I just stare into his eyes as he showcases himself to me? This is probably the most vanilla strip tease known to man, but I'm reacting like I'm in heat.

He flexes his hands, which are now free from the restraints of his gloves. The tendons in his thick forearms dance under his skin. I'm instantly reminded of when they were wrapped around my waist. I divert my gaze before my mind summons thoughts that would send me straight to the pits of hell.

He lays his gloves and jacket on the chair that has remained in the same position since the other night. He doesn't remove his helmet and walks to the coffee station, leading me to believe that he really meant it when he said he wasn't going to take it off.

"Why don't you take your helmet off too?" I suggest in a joking manner, seeing if he'll actually do it. "It looks heavier today, it's even got a camera on it." I wave at the tiny square device on his helmet when he turns to face me.

"It's not recording, you gotta click this button here." Leaving the coffee to fill, he points to a button on top of the camera.

"Very cool, you should still take off the helmet."

"Now where's the fun in that, Violet?"

"Lots of fun. I would be able to see what you look like, and I can also stop talking to my reflection." I'm surprised by how at ease I am with him. The last time we spoke, he managed to soften me up *a lot*. However, I'm still a little confused about my feelings toward him.

I could leave this job and never see him again; he'd be no more than some customer I joked around with. Because of this, the intensity of my crush has me questioning why I feel so strongly about him. It would've been much easier to forget about him if he didn't keep popping up every few days to flirt with me.

"No. Can I get ten on—"

"Pump two, sure. You get down gas fast," I interrupt.

"I like biking all night, you should join me." I look outside at his bike that sits menacingly on its own in the parking lot.

"I'm good, thanks."

He fetches his coffee and places it down to pay a little too aggressively. The bottom of the cup bends, and it tips unsteadily. The weight of the liquid causes it to topple over. I jump back to avoid the scalding drink and frantically look around the counter for napkins.

"Fuck," he mumbles, picking up the now-empty cup. The way he says the word has me faltering, effectively distracting me in my search for napkins. I only find a small handful of them behind the counter, which is not enough to clean up the spill.

"I'll get some stuff to clean up with, hold on." I walk to the utility closet and prop the door open so I can see. I reach up to get some more napkins. I'm too short, so I stand on my tiptoes to nudge them to the edge of the shelf with my fingertips.

So close!

I let out a strained grunt as I stretch a little further. A loud thud sounds from behind me, and I'm enveloped in complete darkness.

I used an unopened paint can to hold the door, only a person moving it would've caused it to move. Unless there's a very strong ghost haunting the old gas station, it's just Biker Guy and me here.

"Not funny!" I shout. Thankfully, this closet doesn't have an automatic lock, but I can't see what I'm looking for now.

"What's not funny?" A breath tickles my ear. I scream, throwing a weak, reactionary punch straight into a hard body.

Yep, definitely not a ghost.

"Fuck! What is your issue?!" My heart pounds from fright, and arousal starts to seep in from Biker Guy's close proximity. I place both hands on him in a poor attempt at forming some distance between us, my palms flush against his chest. I can't see anything aside from a broad, dark frame that moves closer and pushes me gently against the shelves. I graze my hands over his chest and up to his face to feel him out in the dark. No helmet?

"You took off your helmet?" I ask, a little astonished.

"I did." I feel around some more and find that he's got some sort of material covering everything but his eyes.

"I feel fabric. Do you have a mask on?"

"Yeah, a ski mask. Keeps my face warm when I'm riding." I rub my finger over the ski mask, taking in the hardness of his nose and the length of his jaw. Then, I lean into his neck and smell him. "Did you just smell me?" He lets out a low, husky chuckle.

He smells divine, apart from the off-putting scent of cigarette smoke on his clothes.

"I'm feeling confident in the dark. There's less pressure when I don't have to look at your face and you can't see mine either," I admit.

"I'm feeling confident too."

"As you said when you walked in today, you always feel confiden—"

"Violet," he whispers, his voice gravelly.

"What?"

Something presses against my lips. I'm being kissed.

This unknown customer is kissing me in the utility closet at my job and I don't care.

I open my lips a little, and he uses his tongue to gently caress the inside of them. He must've moved the bottom half of the ski mask to kiss me. I use my hands to feel across the skin of his jaw. It's rough like he hasn't shaved for a few

45

days.

I crave more than just a gentle kiss from this man. It's unclear whether he's being cautious, but I want him to know that I hunger for his lips. I decide to take control and push my tongue into the guy's mouth, attempting to set the pace until he bites my lip in warning.

When I moan, he uses it as an opportunity to match my hunger.

I try to move forward and he holds his ground. It causes us to press against each other instead. I feel something hard against my front, a low noise reverberating in his throat as we devour each other. With one of his large hands, he gathers my much smaller ones behind my back. The other grips the nape of my neck and caresses upward, unclipping my hair and fisting it tightly.

Our kiss is rough, sweet, and everything in between. A result of our unceasing flirting and obvious attraction to each other.

I release my hands from his grip and trail them all over his body, mapping every curve and contour with a fierce desire to memorize every inch.

"You're so eager, Violet," he says against my lips. I respond with an agreeing '*hm*'. He cups my face and pushes me harder against the shelf, causing it to wobble. That's when I feel something light flutter around me.

The napkins.

His lips leave mine, and his tongue and teeth ignite a trail of sensations along my skin when he traces a path down my neck. His affectionate, yet rough, nips at my throat are followed promptly by his return to my mouth. Every touch of his lips feels like a scorching mark on my body; it emits the same heat that courses through my veins and threatens to consume me entirely.

A sudden ring from the bell has me pulling away from him, but his hands stay firmly on the sides of my face. It takes a moment for him to pry himself away.

Our breathing is rapid, like we've done way more than

kissing. I quickly smooth down my hair, gulping a few times to rehydrate my dry throat. I try to compose myself as I gaze at his dark silhouette, and I feel a finger stroke my face—a gentle gesture that brings me back to reality.

With a sharp exhale, I sink down to feel for the napkins until I have a handful of them. I leave Biker Guy behind in the closet, and I don't look back. The cold air from the refrigerators hit my now-damp panties as I walk past them. It causes the memory of the kiss to repeat in my head...I'm still turned on. Why am I still turned on?

I take a large gulp of air before addressing the customer and apologize for the spill. I also notice that Biker Guy has placed his helmet out of the way and under the counter.

I serve the customer in a daze, his eyes regarding me in a way that makes me feel dirty. I feel paranoid interacting with him after what I've just done, it's like he knows exactly what I've been up to in the closet. If I thought I felt unsettled before, he gives me a strange, almost creepy look as he leaves. *Ew.*

Biker Guy approaches me with cleaning cloths. His black ski mask maintains his anonymity, and I still can't make out his face.

Green eyes glaze over when he lowers his gaze to stare at my neck. I touch where he's looking and can't feel anything. I observe him with suspicion, but he looks away to focus a little too intently on wiping the counter. *Is there something on my neck?*

I pull out my phone and open the camera application, tilting my head up to notice a huge red splotch forming. No. Multiple red splotches appear on my neck—no wonder the customer looked at me weirdly.

"Are you insane? I work in a customer-facing job!" Biker Guy rubs a hand over his head.

"My bad," he mutters, adjusting himself in his pants. He's *so* not sorry.

I let out an agitated huff and hunt for some concealer. I pray that Freya's left some behind, or it's one of the random things that the gas station sells. I spot a scarf in lost property and whip it around my neck in a panic.

I take the cloth that Biker Guy placed on the counter and use it to finish wiping up the spill. We clean up without exchanging any words until the silence is swiftly interrupted by a voice that resonates with a deep timbre.

"You ever been on a bike before?" Biker Guy asks, cutting through the awkwardness. I snatch the napkins from his hands and throw them in the trash.

"Never."

I rest my hand on my hip, still irritated by the marks he's left on my neck. I'm ready to shut down any idea he has about me riding a bike. Though I am a bit curious about what it'd be like to sit behind him on a motorbike, our bodies pressed together as the wind—

"Do you have work tomorrow?" he asks, disrupting my thoughts. I pinch the bridge of my nose in a measly attempt at controlling myself, noticing that his tone doesn't seem to allow for any argument.

"I don't have work tomorrow, it's my day off." He nods.

"Perfect, I'll pick you up from your place at midnight. I'm taking you to a race." I forgot that he knows where I live because he followed me home. I'm not sure if I'm naive or just have a huge crush, but I feel strangely safe around him. I'm totally looking past the red flag being waved directly in front of me. This guy has followed me home, and now he's mentioning a midnight bike race. Alarms should be blaring at this point. *Aren't humans meant to have survival instincts?*

"Midnight? That sounds sketchy, plus, I might be busy hanging out with friends." I'm lying. At most, I'll be watching some lame show with my little brother and eating takeout.

Though the idea of riding a bike is an instant no, part of me feels like it would be good for me to do something outside of my comfort zone. Kissing a customer at work was already too much. Riding his bike is just another thing that's out of my range of field, yet somehow feels even more exciting.

"Cancel it," he snaps.

"I'm sure you have other people who are more willing to go to a midnight race with you," I say, trying to sound unbothered.

"I don't want to take anyone else, Violet. You're the only person I want on the back of my bike." His words make my heart stutter. I remind myself that I need to stay focused and not get caught up in this crush. This is a customer, after all. The kiss was a small mistake, he totally caught me off guard. Even though I reciprocated...and would do it again, maybe.

"I'll think about it," I reply, trying to maintain some semblance of rationality.

"I need a straight answer, yes or no," he says, his impatience starting to show.

"It's not just about the bike, it's the race itself that worries me. It sounds dangerous, and I don't want to get into any trouble," I explain. He's asking me out *and* he's getting annoyed that I'm still deciding if I want to go? Rude.

"You're too old to get into trouble," he replies dismissively.

"I'm only twenty-one. I think most people would still be scared of consequences," I retort, watching as he puts on his jacket.

"Not me." He pulls out a pack of cigarettes from his pocket.

"Yuck, clearly." My words are laced with obvious disgust as I eye up the packet in his hand. He tilts his head and squints at me before walking outside. His back is turned toward me to avoid showing the bottom half of his face when he lifts his mask to smoke.

After finishing, he walks to his bike. *Okay, bye then*. I look at the counter to make sure the coffee is cleaned up and notice that he's left his helmet. I grab it and run outside, moving faster when I hear him turn on his bike.

"Hey! Your helmet!" I shout over the sound of the engine, jogging up to his bike. He revs it and looks down toward his back wheel where I see his packet of cigarettes sandwiched between the tire and the ground. He revs again. This time, his back wheel spins on the spot and shreds the packet of cigarettes.

A cloud of smoke fills the parking space, and the scent of burning rubber attacks my nose. It makes me cough until the bike shuts off a few seconds later.

Biker Guy gets off and takes three big steps toward me, his tall frame causing me to look up at him.

"Why did you—"

"I decided to quit," he says matter-of-factly. I shove his helmet into his chest.

"All it took was littering and a destroyed tire, you're so dramatic," I snark. He grabs his helmet and tilts his head back in response to my snappiness. His throat bobs and I stare at it, swiftly averting my gaze when he lowers his face to mine so that our noses are almost touching.

"Worth it. See you at midnight, Sweetness," he hums.

Before I can argue, he puts the helmet on and rides off, leaving me to stare at the destroyed packet of cigarettes on the ground.

Chapter 5

Violet

As my younger brother and I sit on the couch watching some old cartoon show, a familiar rumble echoes through the lounge. It draws both of our attention, and Ash whips his head around in the direction of the noise.

"What the fuck is that?" he asks, turning back to face me.

"Ash! Language," I scold, shaking my head. Ash may be thirteen, but to me, he's still a baby—a very rowdy, potty-mouthed baby.

"What? You know Mom and Dad don't care about cursing," he says, walking up to the window. He's not wrong. Our parents are laid-back when it comes to parenting. While they were stricter with me, Ash seems to get away with anything and everything. You'd think he hasn't been told off a day in his life.

"Why is there a biker outside of our house?" Ash asks with his nose now pressed against the glass.

"It's my friend. I'm going out tonight."

"You? Going out at night?" Ash says dramatically, turning and slapping his hand over his mouth.

"Yes, idiot." I throw a cushion at his head as I stand up from the couch.

"Ouch, violent Violet."

"I'm leaving. Try not to stay up too late," I remind him. Our parents are both pilots, which means that their work schedules are all over the place. They're already fast asleep for the night, so I'm the only person awake to make sure Ash goes to bed.

"Yeah, yeah," he says indifferently, switching on his video game console. "Have fun, Vi." I can't be bothered to argue and give him a pointed look.

When I shut the front door, I instantly notice Biker Guy leaning on a black and red bike instead of his usual all-black vehicle.

"New bike?" I ask as I walk up to him, trying to hide my nerves. He gives a slow sweep of my body, causing me to heat up under his gaze.

"No, this is my fast one," he says, standing up and grabbing a helmet from the back of it. Trepidation sweeps through me as I step closer to him.

Instead of his usual plain leather jacket, he's donning a

black baseball jacket with sewn-on patches, along with jeans and a black muscle top. He looks good, to put it lightly.

"Two helmets. Nice to see you being safe." I hold my hands out, and he places the helmet into my extended arms. I assess it by checking for cracks, dents, and anything that might be a safety issue.

"You're the safest you'll ever be with me," he says, crossing his arms and watching me continue my examination of the helmet. "Put it on, Violet. I'll wait here all night if I have to." I huff in frustration. He tilts his head as if he's either daring me to disobey or is humored by my pedantic behavior.

I place the helmet roughly on my head and fiddle with the buckle underneath. Biker Guy lets out a laugh and impatiently uses his gloved hands to buckle it for me. He taps my chin when he's done, the action feeling oddly intimate.

"Wasn't that hard was it, Sweetness?"

"It was the most difficult thing I've ever done in my entire life," I say sarcastically.

"Get on, I ride safe." He puts on his helmet and slaps the end of the seat before straddling the bike. I have about fifty questions regarding my safety on this thing, and I don't doubt that he would wait all night until I got onto the bike.

I copy him warily and settle onto the bike less than gracefully. The cargo pants that I wore with the intention of being practical uncomfortably shift into less desirable places. Biker Guy settles himself in front of me, and I wrap my arms around him, keeping some distance between my front and his back.

He's broad, so it's a little hard to hold him tight and stay a respectable distance away. I switch hand positions a few times to get more comfortable. First on his shoulders, then around his torso before placing them on his shoulders again.

He suddenly turns on the engine, accelerates, and brakes sharply. The bike jolts. I shriek as I'm thrown forward against his back, grunting when I bash against his body. My arms latch around him in response. He then reaches his arm back to pat the edge of my thigh and squeeze it before taking off.

I don't know what's vibrating more violently, me or the bike. The pat on my thigh has sent my brain into overdrive, and being plastered to his back means that I can barely focus on the ride. My eyes are closed for most, if not all, of the journey—a combination of fright from the high speeds and being so turned on.

I silently will myself to focus on anything other than this man in front of me.

His body shields me from the wind as it whips around us, and I only open my eyes whenever we slow down. Each time I open them, the surroundings become more unfamiliar. It feels like way more than an hour until we slow down almost completely.

We ride through a forest, the gaps between the trees large enough to weave through. Driving at high speeds for so long clearly has us in the middle of nowhere.

Biker Guy pulls up to a dark parking lot. I can hear the

deep, thumping bass of music playing ahead, and we move slowly through some more trees before we reach a large clearing that looks like some sort of race track. People are dotted between bikes, chatting in groups and laughing amongst themselves.

The clearing starts to fill with different types of bikes, their riders doing various tricks and kicking up powdery dirt in the process. Loud revs sound from every direction. Rather than a race, this appears to be a mass bike meet-up.

We stop a fair distance from the crowd, and I strategically slide off the bike to avoid falling off and making a fool of myself. He rises from his bike and takes off his helmet, approaching me where I stand as I struggle to unclip my own.

He uses a finger to hook through the belt loop on my pants and pulls me toward him. His hands hold my hips to prevent me from colliding into his front. He then reaches up to grip both sides of my helmet, tipping my head back to unclip the buckle under my chin. It's removed along with the scarf that I've kept around my neck all day.

Skimming his masked lips over the largest red blotch on my neck, he tucks the scarf into his pocket. I gasp and step back, only for him to hook my belt loop again and pull me back into him.

"Stop moving." The words are hushed, a gentle command that causes my skin to prickle.

He dips his head under my chin once more, his hand reaching under to mess with his mask. I then feel the softness of his lips against the skin of my neck. His tongue tastes me before sucking over the same spot he claimed in the utility closet—a gesture that's a mixture of tenderness and playful intimacy.

"Don't hide your neck. You enjoy showing your artwork and I enjoy showing mine," he murmurs against my throbbing skin.

I thought riding behind him was hot, but his light touches and need to showcase his marks on me have me utterly wound up. If he kisses me now, I might unravel completely.

He fiddles with his mask and then pulls away from me, his face covered.

"How was the ride?" he asks, green eyes sparking with interest.

"Fine," I respond, my voice hoarse. He lets out an amused huff and brings his face close to mine.

"Just fine? I don't like that answer."

I roll my eyes at his words. "You drive too fast. Maybe someone else here can take me on a ride whilst you race. Then I'll let you know how much I enjoy riding a bike without a maniac in control." I let out a laugh to let him know that I'm joking. He pauses, hand gripping his helmet so tight that I think it'll crack.

"Don't mention getting on another man's bike in front of me, Violet. You ride with me, you stay here with me and you leave with me." I glower at his possessiveness; his direct words have me torn between running away from him and jumping him. "Stay next to that white van. Do not move and keep away from the track," he warns, slipping on his helmet.

As soon as he's settled back onto his bike, he gives me one final look before snapping down his visor. He revs his engine so that the crowd parts, allowing him to ride onto the track.

I can feel his annoyance at my joke about riding with someone else, and I try not to dwell on it as I search for the white van.

Finally catching sight of it, I step purposefully toward the vehicle. A man stands on top of it with a large speaker, and a group of women are gathered nearby. I don't recognize anyone. Biker Guy also seems to have completely disappeared into the sea of riders. Damn. I really hope he's not feeding me to the wolves.

The loud noises of the bikes racing down the track make it difficult to focus, and I rub my ears to ease the discomfort. Dim, flickering lights around the track cast an eerie glow on the riders as they show off their skills on the wide concrete stretch. Some ride on one wheel, while others stand on their seats, their figures illuminated by the headlights of their bikes.

"Woah," I mumble.

"Your first race?" I spin to face a beautiful girl. She has long, dark braids and is wearing a black and yellow, oversized leather jacket.

"Can you tell?" I smile at her nervously. Upon arrival, I was convinced that this was more of a bike meet-up than a race, but I guess it's both.

The girl sports a pleated denim skirt and a pink V-neck sweater, which seems out of place paired with the jacket. The amount of blush on her face only adds to her otherwise preppy look, she looks almost fae-like. She's also looking at me curiously, and I notice a large camera sitting around her neck. Maybe she's creative too?

I already feel a little relieved that there's somebody here that may be somewhat similar to me.

"Can I tell? You look like a lost puppy. I'm Mari." She holds her hand out and I shake it a little too firmly. "I'm watching my boyfriend race. This is where the girlfriends stand, left of the van. Well, that's what my man told me. Is your guy racing too?" Mari's voice is soft and calming, a small sense of peace in this new, chaotic environment.

"I'm Violet and no, I don't have a boyfriend." She looks confused and studies my face until her eyes land on my neck. *Fuck.*

"Riiight," she drawls, her glossed lips twitching. "How long have you been together?"

"We're not together," I respond firmly.

"Damn. This guy mauls your neck and trusts you to come to a race despite not being together? Strange relationship." She scrutinizes me like I'm lying. "This is my second time here, and I've been with Isaac since middle school. He wouldn't let me come to a race for *years*."

If Mari is shocked that I'm here based on my lack of

relationship status, then I'm not making it known that I don't even know my biker's name…or face.

Dread settles in my stomach when I realize that I'm at some sort of midnight race in the middle of nowhere with a guy whose physique I am more familiar with than the entirety of his face.

It's like our odd situation is normalized between us, only for me to realize how strange it truly is when conversing with other people.

Mari is quickly distracted by the bikers and uses it as an opportunity to get some shots. I watch her for a short while as she captures images of the bikers in action, then I decide to walk off to wander along the edge of the track. I pass by the remains of a fence with a disintegrating poster, nervously nibbling at the loose skin around my nails.

After around twenty minutes of being repeatedly startled by the random backfiring of bike engines, a piercing sound screeches around us. Bright flood lights turn on and bathe the race track in industrial lighting.

Upon further inspection, it's an abandoned runway. I'm not aware of there being one near where I live. Where the fuck am I?

I walk back to Mari, who is now my unofficial comfort person after being the only one I've spoken to in this unfamiliar space. I watch a guy on a bike drive up to the edge of the track where a girl is standing. He leans forward on one wheel to pass her a rose before speeding off.

"What if they get caught racing?" I ask, fully aware that this is more than likely an illegal race.

"By who? The cops? We're more likely to get caught, they'd have to catch the bikers first. Plus, no license plates make it more difficult." She gestures at the runway as another pair of bikes zoom past. Mari and I watch the bikers for a while until a loud voice booms from the van next to us.

"Good evening, ladies and gentlemen!"

Shouts and whistles sound from around the track with people scurrying to secure places along the outside length of the runway.

"I've been told that the cops are on their way as usual, which means we only have time for one major race tonight," the guy on top of the van thunders. A chorus of boos sound in response to his announcement. "Now, now. It's not my fault. We are no strangers to this type of interruption."

"Fuck the police!" some guy shouts from across the track, causing a few people to laugh.

"Exactly," the speaker guy agrees, pointing in the direction of the shouting man. "Which is why we do our polls to decide who will be racing."

Some girl behind Mari and I grumbles to her friends about favoritism. Mari turns to glare at her, and the girl looks at Mari's jacket. She smirks and whispers something to her friend.

The MC starts calling out names for each of the selected riders, and several bikers head to the starting line.

"They usually do street races, but this is the first time in a while they're using this old runway. The cops haven't anticipated this being used again. We are so far away from the nearest town, that if the cops find out about the race, it takes them a while to get here. They don't know the shortcuts to the track," Mari explains.

Well, that doesn't sound very reassuring.

"How long do we have until they get here then?" I ask, my nerves knotting in my stomach.

"Well, the MC said that we only have time for one race until we see the blue lights. We probably only have an hour, if that. They do a poll on social media before every race night so that if the races are cut short, the most anticipated riders are prioritized." This seems very planned out, and my complete lack of knowledge puts me on edge.

"Isaac is in the yellow, he is usually selected," Mari says, pointing down the long stretch. I can't see anyone specific from this far away because we are closer to the end of the track.

I have no idea how, or if, she can see anyone from this distance. I don't even know if Biker Guy is racing. Despite waiting for several minutes, he still hasn't appeared.

"Alright, let's get this show on the road!" the white van guy shouts. The whistles and whoops get louder, and Mari grabs my hand, squeezing it tight.

As much as I hate to admit it, the nerves in my stomach merge with excitement, and the revving sounds have me sucking in deep breaths of air. I thought the bikers were still getting ready to race, but the sound of rubber on asphalt suddenly ensues.

I see several bikes speeding toward us, the riders becoming clearer in their approach. I am able to see the yellow biker that Mari pointed out. She takes several pictures and whoops—her soft shout is no match against the deafening roar of the bikes.

I'm convinced I can see a familiar red and black bike in third place. With no sign of Biker Guy, I'm assuming it's him.

The bikes go past so fast, that if I blinked or looked away even for a second, I would've missed them passing me. Heads snap as the bikes zoom by, and people start running after them. I'm sure Biker Guy was in third.

I seek out Mari who begins to follow the crowd that's heading to the finish line, probably to find her guy.

I debate between hanging near the van or following the crowd. Biker Guy's firmness about me staying near the white van has me rooted in place—he doesn't seem to play around when it comes to my safety.

"First place, Dynamite Devon!" the MC shouts. "Isaac second and Tino third!" I listen as the MC rattles off a few other names, some nicknames cheesier than others. When I watch him stand on top of the van from his seated position, concern shows on his face. He's spotted something.

"Lights! Fifteen minutes!" he shouts into the mic, jumping

down from the tall vehicle and packing the speakers away.

Several hordes of people start running into the forest and others, seemingly unfazed by the cops, chat with the racers.

Everything is happening so fast, but the third place name remains ringing in my head. Tino.

Mari is walking ahead, and she halts a little when she sees that I'm still where I was standing during the race.

"C'mon!" she yells, beckoning me with her hand. I shake my head.

"I'll hang back!" I shout over the crowd. She gives a small wave before heading to the racers.

My eyes zone in on one familiar biker who marches past Mari with his bike in tow, heading straight toward me. Mari smiles and gives me a thumbs-up.

"Well done, *Tino*," I say when he's within hearing distance. I emphasize his name, and he pulls off his helmet to reveal the ski mask.

"Wrong name, Sweetness." Surely not.

"What? You came third…right?"

"I never lose, Violet," he says as if it's common knowledge. If he came first, then he would be…

Dynamite Devon.

"Devon," I breathe. His eyes light up and then darken when I reach out to touch him.

"Yo, Devon!" I don't have time to bask in the glory of knowing his name because he's almost pushed forward into me, the movement causing him to let go of his bike.

Devon only budges slightly and turns to look at who I presume is Isaac in the black and yellow leather.

"You're a fucking fraud," Isaac growls at Devon. They're both around the same height, but Isaac somehow looks slightly childish compared to Devon's domineering figure. I see Mari hovering behind Isaac, and she gives me a sad smile.

"What's your problem, Isaac?" Devon looks at Mari who gives a small shrug back, almost like they're both familiar with Isaac's antics.

"You're the problem. That was my fucking win!" Isaac shouts, looking like he's about to spit venom. A crowd begins to form around us.

"Clearly not," Devon says as if Isaac is boring him.

Mari steps forward and tries to pacify her boyfriend. "Devon won fair and square, babe."

"Shut the fuck up, Mari," Isaac hisses. I've only just met Mari, but I have a need to stand up for her.

I cut into the conversation, my words dripping with fury, "Don't speak to her like that." Isaac whips his head to me, as if he's only just realized I'm there.

"Got yourself a little supporter, hm?" Isaac smirks at Devon and then directs his gaze to my neck, moving toward me.

"Take one more step forward and I'll break your foot. I've done it before," Devon cautions.

"And I'll have you arrested and thrown behind bars, again." Devon's been arrested for hurting someone? The

66

crowd around us jitters with excitement, clearly finding the whole ordeal entertaining.

"Fuck off, Isaac. If you're done here, we're leaving," Devon says through gritted teeth and leans down to pick up his bike. Isaac suddenly rushes forward with a yell and swings at Devon, catching him in the jaw. Devon retaliates by throwing a combination of punches. He lands every one of them.

Mari screams as Isaac's fist skims past Devon's face. The ski mask shifts a little. It's not enough for me to see any more of his face, but enough that if his hair was long it would've shown.

Everything happens so fast, and some guys rush in to stop the fight. They're too slow because Devon catches Isaac around the face and directly on the nose.

"Motherfucker!" Isaac roars, holding his face as blood begins to stream through his fingers.

Devon grabs me along with his bike and walks to the tree line at the edge of the runway. Animosity radiates off him in waves. I look behind at the scene and see Mari rushing up to Isaac who gives her a look that has her cowering back.

"Keep walking, Violet," Devon says, noticing my steps falter.

Another girl rushes to Isaac's side, he doesn't resist when she takes his face in her hands. Mari looks pained and my heart aches for her. Devon sets up the bike and motions at me to put on the helmet. He nudges me gently toward the vehicle, pulling my attention away from Mari.

As we prepare to leave, I notice that most of the spectators have already dispersed. This is fortunate because I can spot cops emerging from the overgrown entrance of the runway. My heart races so fast that it's almost painful, the gravity of the situation settling in.

"Devon…" I say cautiously.

"Hold tight Violet, we're cutting it close."

Chapter 6
Violet

Devon navigates us flawlessly, and we surge through the trees until we emerge onto a main road. I let out a breath of relief, which is interrupted when a siren suddenly sounds from behind us.

I turn to see a cop car tailing us. Devon also looks over his shoulder and shakes his head in what looks to be annoyance rather than fear. All my doubts prior to going to this race play on a loop through my head, and I feel like my hesitance to come in the first place is biting me in the ass.

Body tense, Devon leans forward and accelerates. I bury my face into his back and open my eyes when I feel the bike tilt low before straightening again.

The bike moves like that several times, my adrenaline

rising with each dip. Devon quickly puts distance between us and the cop car, which can't keep up with the bike's speed.

He makes a right down a narrow path that's too tight for a car. The turn is so sharp that dirt kicks up against my leg as Devon uses his foot to help us pivot.

We continue down the forest trail, and Devon turns off the engine as soon as we're far enough from the main road. As if rehearsed, he lifts me off the bike and shoves it into a ditch.

"What—" I barely begin my question because Devon grabs me. We follow the bike down a steep decline until we're nestled out of sight. He lays me on top of him and holds me tight against his front, the position uncomfortable with a bulky helmet on.

I feel a little nauseous, unable to stop shaking. Devon rubs my arm as if attempting to soothe me, my muscles aching from lying so stiff.

I hear loud footsteps above us, and I hold my breath. After what feels like ages, the words "*too dark*" and "*not worth it*" are muffled before fading as if the people talking are moving away. I don't move an inch until we hear a car driving off.

Devon slowly untangles himself from me and helps me up, placing me gently on a nearby log. Whilst he goes to grab his bike, I take off my helmet and suck in a deep breath.

Holy shit.

"You okay?" I ask Devon, who has also taken his helmet off. I walk up to him and place a hand on his back. He stiffens at my touch and turns to me once the bike is propped up.

"I would've killed Isaac if he touched you," he seethes. *What? Where is this coming from?*

"You're thinking about that douchebag when we nearly just got caught by the cops?" I ask, breathing out an exasperated laugh.

"Yes, is that a problem?" His tone is condescending, as if my confusion isn't justified. Now, I'm also angry. My anger is combined with every other intense emotion that has been bubbling at the surface since I entered that abandoned runway.

I'd even argue that I've been brewing since Devon and I's kiss, though I felt much less hostile than this.

"Yes, it is a problem because you're acting like this when I don't even know you!" I shout, the volume of my voice increasing by the last word.

Birds fly out of some nearby trees, and Devon just looks at me in silence through his mask. His eyes are unreadable, concealing any trace of emotion. Why does that make me angrier?

I can't even look at him to decipher his reaction because I can't see his face with his stupid mask on. The only thing I'm sure about is that Devon's mad about some guy called Isaac because he moved a little closer to me than he would've preferred.

"Feel better now?" he asks with a voice that is annoyingly calm. His response being another question sends me over the edge. With the stress of tonight, my words escape me.

"Why are you upset that Isaac spoke to me? He didn't even touch me, Devon. I think this is all becoming too much." His eyes cut to mine, confusion settling in his gaze through the fabric of his ski mask. "We barely know each other. I don't even know what you look like."

I start pacing, my feet crunching against the dried leaves and twigs on the forest floor.

"I almost got caught by the cops. I mean, shit, I don't know why I thought this was a good idea. I don't think I was even thinking." I feel frustrated. Partly at Devon, but mostly at myself. "You're practically a stranger," I say, ending my short tangent.

Devon watches me like one would assess a feral animal before deciding to approach it. It's obvious that the adrenaline hasn't left my body.

He closes his eyes slowly, trying to compose himself. "It wasn't me following you home that was the line?"

"This was the wake-up call, you're still a stranger."

He exhales loudly and strides toward me, yanking me into his body. The heat of his hand radiates against where he holds the nape of my neck, his lips providing a similar warmth as they rest against my ear.

"Let me ask you something, Violet. You'd let a stranger kiss you at work?"

"Well, no but—"

"You'd let a stranger pick you up at midnight to take you to an illegal race? You could've stayed home." I could've, but I didn't.

"I just—"

"You place an awful lot of trust in a stranger, Sweetness." My body is tight, and Devon's hand circles the front of my throat. A firm, yet gentle grasp on my neck that causes me to suck in a shaky breath.

I like the feel of his hand secured around my throat. It's not violent or scary…it's erotic and possessive. A firm hold that mimics the one he has on my volition.

"This isn't me, all of this is reckless," I argue weakly, leaning into his touch.

"I don't think I'm a stranger to you, Violet. I can see the way your thighs clench and release as if they don't ache to wrap around my head every time you hear my voice."

Devon's thumb rubs up and down my throat, trailing the movement of the muscles as I painfully swallow in response to his words.

I have nothing left to argue.

We could go back and forth all day, battling between my desires and my doubts.

It's not just that he has a point, but I have the stark realization that compared to the first time we met, he's more of a friend than a stranger.

He's somebody that knows me, knows my body, and knows how much I want him. My denial is futile, but fighting against my feelings makes me feel like I have some sort of control.

Devon clicks his tongue in thought.

"Sure, you're being a little reckless…but it's all been your choice, hasn't it?" He pauses when I don't respond. "You know what? Why don't I take those choices away from you for a little while? I'll show you something reckless right now, but it'll be on *my* terms."

I remain silent and he lets go of my neck, the cold air hitting the space his hand once occupied. Part of me wants to reach out and attach it permanently around my throat like a necklace.

"Straddle the bike," he instructs. I hesitate slightly, not expecting him to ask that of me.

"I—"

"Straddle. It." With arousal, denial, and adrenaline coursing through my veins, I'm moving like I've been hypnotized. I walk to the bike and straddle it. "Face me," he orders. I follow the sound of his voice and spin so I'm still straddling the bike, my back facing the handles.

Devon walks up to me and runs his hands down my body, pushing on my shoulders so I'm leaning back on the bike. His hands brush over my nipples and my back arches. "Does this feel like a stranger's touch to you?" I shake my head as his thumb runs lightly over my breasts again. "Speak to me."

"You're not a stranger, Devon." He hums his approval and pinches my nipple, twisting it in a way that causes a delightful pain.

It elicits a gentle, fluttering sensation within my chest. That fluttering continues down my body and across the band of my pants, following the path of his fingers.

"Up," he says.

"Up?" I breathe, lifting my head up to see what he's talking about.

"Your hips. Up." I do as he says and lift them.

In one swift movement, he yanks my pants and underwear down my legs. I gasp as the night air hits my bare skin. It cools the space between my legs—a space which his eyes seem to be glued to.

He walks around the bike like he's analyzing me, my eyes following his movements as his weighty stride echoes through the woodland. He stops and crouches so that his eyes are level with my pussy.

"You're already dripping…the only thing I've done is hold your neck. I haven't even touched you here yet."

He reaches out and rubs his finger lightly over my clit. I'm already so worked up that my hips jolt. I grip the leather of the seat to stabilize myself in fear that the more he touches me, the more likely I am to fall off the bike.

His finger moves to my hole and it enters me a little before retreating. Dragging my wetness over my clit, he circles it before dipping back into my pussy. My body heats as I'm worked up more and more.

Dip, stroke up, circle. Dip, stroke up, circle.

His rhythmic fingers build up my pleasure slowly, and I angle my hips so that he can reach the exact places I want him to. Until he stops.

I let out a shuddering breath and watch as he circles the bike again. He trails his finger across my lips like one would apply lipstick, spreading my arousal over my mouth. My tongue darts out, and I taste myself.

He gives me an approving nod as he lowers himself once again, this time crouching at my hip. His hand grabs my wrist and nudges my pointer finger to straighten it out. He gently shifts his hand to align it with mine, mirroring the placement of my finger.

With his pointer finger now resting on top of my own, he slides our hands down to my lower abdomen, skating down to my clit.

"Look, we're working together like *strangers*," he murmurs, throwing my earlier statement back into my face.

"Devon…" Instead of sounding like a warning, my tone lacks conviction and transforms into a moan.

"How nice, you know your *stranger's* name."

He circles us around my swollen pussy. I'm so wet that our fingers slip over me with ease.

My eyes water in pleasure, and I clamp my bottom lip down with my teeth to stop myself from moaning. Moving us faster over my swollen core, he pushes my hand away so he can massage the flats of four of his fingers over me.

Tension builds and the wetter I get, the faster he moves. My hips lift up, my pussy adhering to his hand like a magnet. I moan and shake, body clenching as my orgasm washes over me.

I'm draped haphazardly over the bike, and I don't have time to reposition myself because Devon lightly swats my still-sensitive clit. I buck so hard that I almost slide off the seat.

With my body hanging off the bike, my head lolls, and my long hair now rests on the forest floor. I have to grab onto the handles to stop myself from slipping off completely.

"Not done yet, Sweetness."

"I can't," I whimper.

"You will."

Now weak from my orgasm, my hand unlatches from the handles. As I'm about to fall, Devon lifts me up and repositions me back onto the bike. He strokes my clit with one finger again and I gasp, covering it with my hands.

Devon bends down to my pussy and places my hands in front of his face, lifting the bottom half of his mask to free his mouth.

My hands obscure his face, and I can't see anything besides what I usually see when he has his ski mask on. If I move them, I will be able to see the bottom half of his face.

It's like he's giving me the power to reveal him.

A power that I refuse to take advantage of by keeping my hands exactly where they are.

"Interesting," Devon purrs.

I watch him lower his face until it's obscured by my thighs. He dips down so his lips graze my wet center, and I place my hands on his head, his face still unrevealed to me.

I don't care about his face right now because with one long swipe of his tongue, he tastes me. I shake from a combination of the cool wind, his mouth and residual sensitivity from my previous orgasm.

I sigh in pleasure when he buries his face into me and focuses his tongue solely on my clit.

He alternates between sucking and licking. I can tell that he's listening carefully to the sounds I make to decide how to use his mouth against my most sensitive spot.

"If this is how wet you get for a stranger, you must be drowning the men you know," he says from between my legs.

I want to tell him that there are no other men and that he's the only person who makes me this wet, but my tight throat prevents my words from sounding.

A thick finger suddenly enters me and I let out a loud whine. He laps at me, my clit bumping against his nose. I look down to where Devon is and meet mossy, green eyes that are trained on me.

He moans into me, and I try to move my hips so I can bring myself to release again. His hands hold me still and he squints at me in warning, digging his fingers into my thighs. His digit curls inside of me and my head falls back. Blood rushes to it, making me more lightheaded than I already am.

"Suck," I rasp. "Yes! Circle it and suck…oh my god…more, Devon."

"Would you fuck a stranger's face like this, Violet?"

"No," I whimper, my thighs trembling and squeezing his head.

"Louder."

"No!" I shout. I don't know what he wants from me. Is he trying to get me to convince myself that he's not a stranger?

I don't think I'd even be in a position to deny it after this.

"Scream it, Sweetness. I want you so loud that the cops will know exactly where we are. Would you fuck a stranger's face like this?"

"NO!" I bellow and let out a sob of complete elation as I topple over the edge for the second time. My nails dig into Devon's scalp through the mask, and he doesn't stop sucking me until I stop twitching. I breathe hard, trying to catch my breath. Devon instantly elevates my head, holding it up until he's sure I won't fall back again.

It takes me a while until my breathing returns to normal and I can sit up on my own.

Devon has readjusted the bottom half of his ski mask like it had never been moved. I jerk once more when he swipes his fingers over my pussy and holds them up to me. His eyes lock onto mine. My cum gleams between his fingers before they disappear under his mask. Then, he moans as he tastes me. Not a small noise of satisfaction…a low, guttural *moan*.

I expect to feel embarrassed, even mortified. But I feel nothing of the sort.

Instead, I feel a carnal longing—as if I want more. With or without the mask, I want Devon to ruin me in the best way possible.

Devon's hand reaches around to grip the back of my head, halting me as I begin to stand. He brings his face close to mine. Close enough that I can smell the hint of mint and my own arousal on his breath, but not close enough that I can taste it.

"Lick it off," he rumbles, his voice almost inaudible.

Devon points to the bike seat which shows my wet release glistening on the dark leather. *He's got to be joking*. His eyes do nothing but harden, and I press my legs together. *He's not joking—fuck*.

Devon lightly pulls my hair, and I bend over the seat. I'm taunted by the wet patch less than an inch away from my nose. My hesitation causes Devon to maintain his hold on my hair and lower himself until his eyes are level with mine.

"We can't ride home on a dirty seat, Violet," he says as if trying to convince me that licking myself off his seat would be beneficial to both of us. Unbeknownst to him, I am more than willing to do this.

My nails dig into the edge of the leather. With my eyes squeezed shut, I stick out my tongue and swipe it over the seat. I hope my face doesn't show how much I'm enjoying this.

"All of it," he demands. I nod, licking the seat with more enthusiasm. "Mmm, isn't that delicious?" I ignore him and he clutches my hair a little harder in warning. This causes my scalp to tingle.

"Delicious," I utter. I don't know what to think, or how to feel. Am I disgusted? Excited? I don't have time to overthink it because Devon pulls me up gently and swipes his thumb across my lips. As if conditioned to do so, I suck his thumb.

"Good girl," he praises.

I guess I am a good girl.

A good girl that went to an illegal bike race, engaged in a police chase, and enjoyed it when a stranger wrapped his hand around her throat. A good girl that also came all over his bike and licked up her own bodily fluid off the seat.

I'm such a good girl.

I don't know how this escalated so quickly. I'm beginning to think that I'm not even trying to prevent things from happening between us. I like to imagine that it's my mind saying no and my body saying yes, but we both know that's not true.

There's not one part of me that is saying no.

I silently move off the bike and get dressed with Devon watching me. If I had a list of things to do before I die, going to an illegal event, getting chased by cops, and public indecency would all be checked off in the space of a few hours. I can't tell if Devon is a bad influence or not.

If he is, I don't seem to mind.

At all.

Chapter 7

Devon

Riding my bike is a great distraction, and it helps me get over things that would otherwise rest heavy on my mind.

Bad day? I'll ride my bike. Watching my favorite F1 team lose? No problem, riding my bike will make me feel better.

Making Violet finish on the seat of my bike? Well, I thought riding would distract me…but I was wrong.

I watch the needle on my speedometer skirt past the one hundred miles per hour mark and stop accelerating when I realize that going any faster isn't going to distract me like it normally does.

I doubt that anything will erase my memory of Violet's body writhing all over my bike. Every time I close my eyes, the image of her is burned into the back of my eyelids.

When she got off my bike and went inside her house, she didn't utter a word. Like a true gentleman, I gave her some space. A week has passed since then, and I'm finding it harder to stay away from her.

She haunts me when I'm not around her. And when I'm with her, she possesses me in every sense of the word.

I am done for.

Her words about me being a stranger make me want to prove to her that I'm anything but. I'm genuinely considering whether I should just take off my mask in front of her.

When I placed her hands in front of my face on the bike, she didn't move them to see my lower face like I expected her to. It was odd. Maybe the pleasure was too much, or she's just really into me being faceless.

Despite her unwavering belief that I'm a stranger, I'm willing to compromise by sharing some information about myself. I know that she's going to like what she sees when my face is revealed, but I'll keep her itching for more of me.

If she's unsure that she wants to see my face, then I'll have her begging for her faceless admirer to show just a little of himself—and I'm going to enjoy every second of it whilst it lasts.

I pull up to the gas station and take off my helmet as I walk through the door. Ski mask on, of course.

Violet doesn't say anything, and I sit in my usual chair. She keeps peering up at me from the price sign she's designing as if debating what to say. She's probably aching to talk about what happened that night on the bike. I'm almost tempted to ask her if I've been on her mind as much as she's been on mine.

"Where did you get the name Dynamite Devon?" I'm relieved to hear her voice, but twist my lips at her reference to my childhood nickname. The name lives on into my adult life and still manages to make me cringe.

"Used to compete in races when I was younger. I'd always make an explosive comeback in the last few seconds, hence the dynamite," I explain. She nods slowly, her pen hovering over the sign.

"Sounds like something my brother would enjoy."

"You have a brother?" For some reason, I assumed she was an only child—it must've been the vibe I got from her when we first met.

"Yeah, he's thirteen. He loves skateboarding and is a menace to society." She chuckles.

"Sounds like me at that age." She ponders over my words, and a more awkward silence ensues.

"So, that Isaac guy got you arrested?" That name coming from her lips is enough to raise the hackles on my back.

"Yeah, aggravated assault. Bailed out by a friend." Regret paints across her face. *Great.* "I was defending myself," I add quickly. Her shoulders sag a little in relief.

"Why were you fighting at all?" she asks, shaking her head in disappointment. I usually don't give a fuck about fighting someone if it's deserved, but Violet almost has me rethinking

85

my actions.

"Isaac has always hated me, ever since school. He's a violent guy and decided that fists were better than words. He hangs out with terrible people too. It seems like the only nice person around him is his girlfriend. She wouldn't hurt a fly, and I don't have a problem with her."

I've seen Mari only a couple of times at the races and occasionally around school back in the day when she was on the track team. She always ran past the tree I hunkered under when I'd wait for Kas to finish his wrestling training.

She never snitched on me when I was smoking a joint there, so I owe her for not getting me kicked out of school.

When she's not at the races, Isaac is constantly flirting with other women. Everybody knows that he cheats on Mari, including Mari. With Isaac noticing Violet at the race, I wouldn't be surprised if she is on his radar. Though, I doubt he'd sniff around her because he knows how I'd react.

"I see," Violet hums, her attention back on the sign.

"You gonna stop with the small talk, Sweetness?"

"I actually enjoy small talk. It's what you do when you get to know someone." She squints at me in judgment and juts her head forward. There it is, her little angry streak.

"Well, we clearly have different approaches to getting to know someone," I joke, partly referring to what we did in the forest.

"Yeah, mine usually starts with a date and seeing the person's face," Violet counters. I wish I found Violet's attitude off-putting, but it's honestly really fucking hot when she talks back to me.

"Fine, since you still seem convinced that I'm a stranger, let's go on a date tomorrow." I rest my forearms on my thighs and lean forward in my seat. She remains silent for a moment, her mouth contorted in a suppressed smile.

If I'm not mistaken, there's a hint of relief on her face. I think Violet is happy that I've asked her out. I also think I might be out of the stranger-zone.

"I'm busy, actually. I have a party to attend with a friend because I have friends to spend my nights with." I notice her little dig at me spending my time coming to the gas station. It doesn't bother me as much as the sound of her going to a party does.

"Party?" Parties mean gross, horny men. I don't want Violet mingling with the likes of those disgusting guys. Ironic, considering I licked and sucked on her until she almost passed out in the middle of a forest, *and* I just admitted to her that I have a criminal record.

"Yeah, I have tomorrow off work and a few days off next week. The party is for a fight or something. My friend's friend, Micah, is hosting it." She pauses her drawing as if she's considering what she's just said, probably caught herself saying too much again. I am always thankful when she overshares. *Always.*

I straighten at the sound of two words: fight and Micah. They click together like a puzzle, and a previous conversation with Kas comes to mind. Violet is going to Micah's party.

"Oh, nice. I'm not familiar, is it local?" The lie slips out of my mouth before I can even attempt to stop it.

"Depends on what you mean by local. Where do you live?"

"Like an hour or so away from here," I say, and her eyebrows raise in surprise.

"You drive an *hour* to come here? There must be multiple, nicer gas stations closer to you."

"Yeah, but the clerk at this one lets me eat her pussy on the back of a bike." Violet's breathing hitches and causes her to choke on air. She sips from a mug to regain control of her coughs.

"Let's just move past what happened, okay?" she says, pressing a hand to her throat.

Move past what happened? I think not.

"You're seriously asking me to move past that? The hottest thing I've ever done with a woman, and you want me to just *move past it*? You expect me to pretend that I'm not a changed man after that?" Violet turns crimson and buries her face into her hands.

"Stop, Devon," she mumbles into her palms.

"Fine." I laugh, itching to taste her on my tongue again.

We sit in painful silence; the only sounds are the buzzing of the overhead lights and refrigerators. I'm not leaving. If we aren't going on a date tomorrow, then I'll bring the date to her now.

I stand up and grab several items from around the store:

iced tea, some cookies, chips, and a coffee cup. Violet's dark eyes watch me suspiciously as she moves the sign off the counter to make room for me to dump the food and drinks.

"Devon, what are you doing?" she asks, twisting her hair up into her signature clip.

I open the chips and fold down the edges of the packet to create a makeshift bowl. I then peel open the box of cookies, pour the iced tea into the coffee cup and push it under the plastic barrier. Reaching behind me, I drag my chair closer to the counter.

I don't intend on eating because of my mask, but I consider this a step forward.

"Let's meet in the middle. I keep my mask on, and you can ask about anything you want to know about me." I gesture to the spread I've created next to the cash register. "Our first date."

"I—"

"If your problem is that you don't know me that well or that we're *strangers*, then you'll get to know me. Eat up." I maintain eye contact with her, silently encouraging her to ask a question. Distracted by her lips, I watch her take small bites out of a chip and swallow before asking a question.

"How old are you?" We're starting from the beginning, I see.

"Twenty-four," I reply. "About to turn twenty-five."

"I thought you were much older than me, like, pushing thirty. But then again, you are quite immature," Violet quips and I open my arms in a playful gesture, accepting the joke.

"You haven't seen my face, and you're judging my age off my behavior so willingly?"

Violet barks out a laugh and rolls her eyes.

"Okay, what's your occupation?"

"Racer and mechanic." Violet looks at me unbelievingly.

"Legal occupation."

"Mechanic."

"Favorite food?"

"Baklava."

Our back and forth starts off snappy until Violet pauses. "Oh my god," she gasps and leans forward in excitement.

"What?"

"I love Baklava," she gushes.

"I'll get you some," I say instantly. I have no idea where I can get Baklava, I haven't had it since I ate it at a Turkish restaurant when I visited Micah in LA.

"You bake?! There's nowhere that sells them locally." Violet's face lights up, a drastic change to her emotions earlier. I don't bake, but her liking the dessert has me wanting to order every piece of baking equipment I can find just to learn.

"No, but I have my sources." By sources, I mean Kas. Kas can do everything. I have no doubt in my mind that if I pay him enough, he will make some.

"I'll believe it when I see it." She grabs a cookie from the packet. "You really aren't going to take off your mask to eat with me on our date?"

"Do you want me to take it off?" I ask, curious to know what her response is.

"Both, but I kind of want to see it off more than on," she admits, and I get it. Too bad, Sweetness.

Suddenly, an idea springs to mind. I'm so proud of it that I'm surprised a lightbulb isn't visible over the top of my head.

"I won't wear a mask the next time we meet. Promise."

"Seriously?" A flicker of enthusiasm flashes across Violet's face.

"Seriously."

I can't tell if the plan I'm forming will completely freak her out, but this party is going to be a lot more fun now that she's going.

"If you're not going to eat then you can help me finish the mural." Violet swallows the rest of her cookie and grabs a chip, walking toward the other side of the store.

She stops in front of a half-painted wall. The top of it is strikingly bare apart from a sketched outline of a cupcake. "I just need you to hold the paint up for me." Violet is completely zoned in on the art, and I'm zoned in on her, entranced by the way she talks about it. "It's such a tiny area, but trying to balance the can while I paint is really difficult."

Violet starts climbing up the unstable ladder, her arm outstretched as she explains. She wobbles, and I lurch out of my seat just as she catches herself. When she takes another step, she moves unsteadily again. I'm out of my seat and grabbing her by the waist.

"I'll paint it," I say whilst holding her steady, her ass directly in my line of sight. She looks down at me, my eyes immediately going to her face.

"I only need you to hold the paint; I can do it myself like I've done the rest," she says pointedly, as if she thinks I'm doubting her ability.

"I love that you paint, and I know that you're capable of handling yourself, but this is dangerous." I push the ladder with the tip of my finger which causes it to teeter on unstable legs. "If I'm here, you're not getting on that ladder." She attempts to climb higher, and I prevent her by gently holding her still. I make a point of gripping her waist tighter in warning so that she gets down.

"Fine, but only because it's safer this way. I will call out instructions from below." We switch places and true to her word, Violet doesn't just call out instructions—she works me like a dog.

With multiple uneven lines fixed and several color changes later, we complete the mural just as the sun begins to rise.

"You do this for a living?" I ask, my arm aching more than after a sparring session with Kas on one of his bad days.

"Yeah, but I take breaks," she says, placing lids back on the paint cans.

"I could've taken a break?" I grit my teeth in pain, rubbing my shoulder. She's brutal.

"Duh, it's tiring work." Violet grins at me, her face

glowing with satisfaction. "But it's worth it. Look at it." She gestures toward the wall we've just finished. "It's like the wall is alive, don't you think?"

It takes me a second to pry my eyes away from her beaming face. I step back to admire the mural in all its glory. The wall is a vibrant explosion of colors and shapes, depicting a collage of food items surrounded by patterns and swirls. The colors are so vivid that they seem to jump off the wall. The details are impressive, and I can't help but be amazed by the way Violet has brought everything to life.

"Yeah, it really does," I agree, feeling a surge of pride welling up within me alongside another raw, overwhelming emotion. That's when I come to a sudden realization: I dislike absolutely nothing about Violet. From her talents and humor to her captivating looks. She is flawless to me.

God, even I'm starting to doubt if it's possible to like someone this fast—I'm not denying it because it feels so right. I wonder if this is how Violet feels too.

I watch her bend down to pick up a can of paint and carry it to the utility closet. I follow suit, picking up the rest of the cans. She props open the door and places the cans down, staring at my arms when she notices me behind her carrying the rest.

"So, you're going to take off your mask for me next time we meet?" she asks excitedly.

I nod, a smile tugging at my lips. "I promised, didn't I?"

"Yeah," she says. She looks at me in conflict like she's

simultaneously thrilled and unhappy that she's going to see my face. Well, at least that's what she thinks.

"It'll be on my terms."

"*Your* terms? Okay…whatever. You're trouble, Devon," she says, arranging the paints.

"Maybe, but you like it." I place my paints on the floor and crowd her in the utility closet. Violet looks up at me with lust-filled eyes. "Close your eyes," I mumble. "Don't open them until I say so." She gives me one thorough look before shutting them, long eyelashes resting on her cheeks.

I pull up the bottom half of my mask and press my lips to hers, feeling the usual shockwave surging between us. Violet's hands wrap around my neck, and I pull her closer by her waist. I suck on her tongue lightly, my lips working with hers. Our teeth clash as we begin to fight for control.

I can feel her body responding to my touch, and I let out a low, throaty noise of desire.

Reaching behind her, I pull her hair loose and massage my fingers against her scalp. She moans in both relief and pleasure, her noises only making me more eager. I don't hold back when I slam her up against the shelves with a force that makes me glad I had placed my hand behind her head to cushion it.

I can almost feel her need for me growing with each passing second, and with every inhale of her sweet scent, I feel my need for her growing too. I trail my nose down her neck and along her collarbone, working my way down her chest until I'm kissing over her clothed breast. Sucking an erect nipple through her thin top, I plaster my face against her, suctioning hard enough for her to squirm.

She's so sweet that if I lick and suck on her too much, I'm worried that she'll dissolve.

"I want to taste you again, you're so fucking sweet," I groan, sucking her harder.

"Then taste me, Devon."

I want to take this further, but not here. I don't know where else though because I want her so badly. All I know is that a gas station isn't the place. I doubt there is an ideal place because when it comes down to it, I'd fuck and eat her pussy anywhere.

I need to leave before I lose control completely. I pull away with my chest tight and heaving.

"You're driving me insane, Violet." My jaw aches with how hard I'm clenching my teeth. I need to get out of this closet.

In fact, I need to get out of this store before I fuck her in here during her shift. "Fuck," I mutter under my breath, my cock desperate to be inside of her.

I feel her rapid breaths against my lips. With her eyes still closed, she leans forward again. I yank myself away from her when our lips brush once more, shoving my mask over my mouth before I get carried away.

"What the fuck, Devon? You're such a tease," she whines. Her forehead creases, and she has yet to open her eyes.

"I'll see you soon, Sweetness," I rasp, resting my covered lips on her forehead. I relish the feel of her body against mine, then swiftly exit the enclosed space. The smell of paint burns my nostrils as I walk out of the building.

I honestly don't know what to do with myself. I've quit smoking because of Violet, so I can't use that as an outlet. I already know that riding does little to keep her out of my head. Now, I just feel guilty for leaving her so abruptly.

I can't help but feel like I'm being driven insane by Violet. The more time I spend with her, the more I'm afraid I'll lose my mind completely.

Her kisses will only satiate me for so long, and I know it's only a matter of time until I'll want her in every possible way.

Chapter 8
Violet

"Straightened or curled?" Freya asks, assessing the flat iron I gave her.

"Hm, curled," I respond from my position on my bed, watching as she takes the scorching hair appliance and wraps a strand of her hair around it.

Freya focuses on curling her hair at record speed while I'm too busy overthinking Devon's last visit. He caught me off guard with his willingness to show his face at our next meeting. Whilst a large part of me can't wait, I'm going to miss the mask.

I don't know why I'm acting like the mask is going to change anything, I was ready to risk it all yesterday. If Devon had told me to bend over in the utility closet last night, I would've done so without a second thought. Mask on and all.

Sighing, I roll onto my back. It's my day off, and that means no thoughts of work. No work means no Devon. I have a party to be excited about instead.

"Freya, do you remember the last party I went to, and I caught my ex cheating?" I say, starting a conversation to distract myself.

"Oh my god! I almost forgot about that. That was the last party you went to? Was it at Micah's too?" Freya gets up and walks over to a small purse where she throws in some lip gloss.

"Yep." I nod. "That was the first time we met, too." My ex was an ass. Looking back at it, I was way too good for him. Stupid high school romance.

Freya hastily slips into a pair of sandal heels and casually pops a piece of gum into her mouth, rushing toward the mirror to quickly assess her makeup.

"Yeah, now we are three years older, single, and going to a party where lots of hot guys will be. Not stupid eighteen-year-olds." She makes a sound of disgust at the last part of her sentence and turns to face me. "Ready?"

"Ready."

We drive to the address, and it surprisingly doesn't take us long to arrive. Stepping out of the car, Freya exudes an air of familiarity as she leads the way. A delicate trace of sweet perfume lingers in the air, trailing after her as we traverse the front yard and move toward a large front porch that's adorned with majestic marble pillars. She navigates us like she's been here a million times before.

"Micah!" Freya calls to the back of a tall guy with curly hair and brown skin. He looks at both of us, and the way he holds himself makes me think he's now a celebrity of some sort. Aside from going to one of his parties before, I don't know anything about him.

Freya mentioned that he's well-known amongst Hollywood cliques. It makes sense. He honestly looks like he should be in clubs, mingling with A-listers; not throwing a party back in his small hometown.

"Hey ladies! I don't recognize you, thanks for coming. What are your names?" He speaks loudly, his voice fighting against the bass emanating from inside the house. He pulls out a phone with a lit up screen showing a list of names and looks up at us expectantly.

"It's me, Freya," she says. Her voice dulls, obviously disappointed that Micah hasn't recognized her. His eyes widen, and he leans forward as if to get a better look at her.

"Freya?" he breathes. "You look…"

"Thanks for inviting us, we're going to head inside. See you around."

"Frey—" Micah doesn't get a chance to finish whatever he was about to say because Freya barges past him.

"God what a fucking ass! I spoke to him so much when he visited the cafe I worked at during high school. I can't believe he didn't recognize me," she rants. "I know I deleted social media, and he hasn't seen what I look like nowadays because we reconnected through text." She stops on the porch and steps to the side to allow some people to walk past us. "But I thought he'd at least recognize me…even with red hair."

"You look a little different since you were eighteen, plus, he's a social guy. You did tell me he was an event planner in LA. Lots of names and faces." Freya seems a little reassured by my response.

She starts to reply, and whatever she is saying immediately turns into white noise. When I look back at Micah's stunned face, my eyes scan the front of the house only to see a vehicle that's lodged deep inside my memory. A red and black motorbike.

A motorbike that I've licked and been licked on.

Devon's here.

He's here, and he probably isn't wearing a mask. What a fucking liar. I told him about the party, and he said he'd never heard of it. I start searching the front of the house from my spot next to Freya, my eyes darting around like a mad woman.

Devon doesn't really stand out when it comes to clothing from what I can tell. I've already seen about five muscular guys in jeans and black tees.

"Hey, you good?" Freya asks, placing her hands on my shoulders and looking into my eyes. "You haven't taken anything, have you?" she asks, a little panicked.

"Just nervous," I say. I'm not lying, I really am nervous about potentially bumping into Devon. It's a party, there's no way he'd have his face covered.

I nervously tuck my hair behind my ear. I did not expect to meet him like this. Is this what he meant when the next time we would meet, he wouldn't wear a mask?

Oh god, I'm spiraling.

"It'll be fine! I'm not drinking, so just let me know when you want to leave," Freya says, completely oblivious to the real reason I'm freaking out. I take a deep breath and force myself to forget Devon for now. Maybe if I forget he's at the party I'll just bump into him naturally.

It'd be like we met here and haven't been having weird masked foreplay the entire time I've worked at the gas station.

I follow Freya into the house, semi-present as she gets talking to some old friends. We dance and socialize for a couple of hours until Freya pulls me to the side for some selfies and group photos.

"Oh my god, why do I look so oily?" I laugh, pinching the screen to zoom into my face.

"It's the flash, everyone looks oily!" Freya snorts as I scroll through the multiple photos she's taken of us with some partygoers photobombing in the back.

"Hey," someone says from next to me. I pause for a moment, and Freya briefly glances at whoever it is. She nods at the guy before moving away after giving me one of those looks that scream, '*I'm here if he does anything weird*'.

I spin to face the guy who's just addressed me. He's kind of cute, actually.

"Hey…" I trail off. Is this Devon? He doesn't sound like him and most definitely isn't as tall as him. *Damn it.* Why isn't Devon falling into my lap?

"Is your name Devon by any chance?" I ask, uncaring of how random my question seems.

"What?" He lets out an uncomfortable chuckle. "No, I'm Vince." Yeah, the more he talks, the less he sounds like Devon—his voice is way too high. I don't want to be rude, but I have no interest in Vince.

"Oh, well nice to meet you, Vince."

Suddenly, a cold splash hits my leg. Vince's glass has been knocked out of his hand, causing some of the liquid to dribble onto my jeans.

"Asshole!" Vince calls out to whoever knocked over his drink. I follow the direction of his shout and notice the backs of several people walking through the crowd. It's a lot busier than when I first arrived, so it's hard to pinpoint the culprit.

"It was nice meeting you Vince, but I think I'm going to clean up." I give him a polite smile and leave our little conversation, knowing full well that the amount spilled on me isn't necessary to wipe up. It landed on my jeans and is barely noticeable.

I make out that I'm leaving to find a bathroom, but circle around until I'm back with Freya.

Even though I've been socializing, my nerves are still high. I have barely been able to hold a decent conversation with Devon constantly swirling around my mind for the entire party.

After thirty minutes, my patience has worn thin. Fuck bumping into Devon naturally...I'm going to hunt him down.

I split from Freya and head upstairs to search for him, even though I don't know what face I'm looking for. He doesn't have any visible tattoos or facial piercings that I know of. He does have short hair, the color of it remains unknown to me, though.

Amidst the dancing guests, I roam aimlessly in search of Devon. My only means of identification being his voice and my intuition. My eyes snap to every ripped guy I see, which is pretty much everyone because it's a post-fight party.

I spot one attractive guy with a huge bruise on his face watching me suspiciously from the top of the stairs. Based on his odd reaction, I would've considered him to be Devon if he wasn't so lean. He looks more athletic than Devon, if that's even possible.

"Hey, have you seen Devon?" I ask as I pass him. He stares at me, then briefly looks behind me. I raise my eyebrow and turn toward the stairs to find nobody there. It's just us here.

"No." He responds dismissively as if I've just inconvenienced him, then walks past me to descend the wide staircase. Clearly, my sleuthing skills need some work.

I walk further down the hallway and run my hand through

my hair in frustration. I keep thinking every guy here is Devon. I'm probably imagining him being here at this point, waiting to eat me out again or something.

I open several doors: a bathroom, a storage room, and another closet with only towels. The next door I open is a bedroom, the light from the hallway illuminating it as I try to locate the light switch. My hand slaps the wall in search of it, which is the moment that someone pushes me in and wraps their arm around my waist.

"Hey!" I shout, kicking my legs and flailing my arms. I'm picked up and carried a short distance onto somebody's lap. The door shuts behind us, and the room is covered in a thick darkness.

"Sweetness." I stop struggling and sag at the sound of the voice, resting myself against the familiar hard body.

"Devon," I mumble into his chest, blindly running my hands over his face. No helmet. No ski mask. My body lights up like a match.

With me currently on his lap, what was initially panic has turned into complete lust. I drag my hands all over his bare face. My fingers graze the sides of his head, and I feel the cold metal of a small hoop earring.

My hands slide over his hair and it's short. So short, that it feels prickly on my palms. He did say that the next time he sees me, he wouldn't wear a mask.

"You kept your promise...you asshole," I whisper. He played me. He kept his promise knowing full well that he wasn't going to show his face.

"But I didn't lie," he says. "No mask."

"You're an idiot." He lets out a rumbling laugh.

"Cute that you were looking for me all night, though."

"It wasn't all night," I argue, trying to squint and see Devon. It's too dark, as usual.

"You nearly passed out when you spotted my bike. I thought I'd have to run in and catch you before you fell."

How long was he watching me for?

"Stalker," I mumble. It's the only comeback my brain can think of, and I shuffle on his lap, gasping when I feel an obvious hardness between his legs.

I think I've been subconsciously conditioned to get turned on by both darkness and Devon, that being the stimulus and my arousal the response.

"I can't tell if that's an insult or not. Last time you called me a name, you came all over my face." I'm almost shaking with arousal on his lap, the chance of potentially seeing him tonight has me all riled up. I lean in and swipe my tongue up the side of his neck. "Violet..." he warns. I drag my lips over his face, brushing them over his stubbled jaw to locate his mouth and kiss him.

I rock my hips, and Devon lets out a low hum. He breaks the kiss by gripping my chin and forcefully detaches his lips from mine.

"Violet, if you don't plan on doing anything more than kissing, you should leave this room." He pulls my face back to his and nips along my bottom lip.

"I want more." I roll my hips over him. The anticipation of bumping into him tonight has acted like my very own foreplay. "Please," I beg.

My skin sizzles under his touch, and I feel like I'm about to detonate. I've given up fighting my body or trying to think what the safest course of action is. All I know is that I want Devon, and I want him now. Even more so after he left me high and dry in the utility closet.

Devon hisses like he's in pain. "If you don't touch my dick in the next few seconds, I'll have to take matters into my own hands." I can feel him throb underneath me. I slide off Devon's lap to kneel in front of him, then I feel my way to his belt.

Just as I locate it, Devon grips my hand and rubs it over his hardness.

"Too slow," he breathes.

Movement ensues, and I hear the telltale sound of a zipper. When I rest my hands on his now bare legs, I lean forward so that my lips meet his dick. I press them lightly against his cock in chaste kisses and my tongue follows. I tease him until he flinches in his seat.

I'm no stranger to giving oral sex, but I never enjoyed it with my ex. With Devon, I have this strange urge to mimic the way he made me feel when he pleased me on the back of his bike. I want to make him lose control in my mouth, and then kiss him so he can savor his own release on my tongue.

I intend to do every filthy, hell-binding act with him. Wherever and whenever.

"You're a fucking dream," he growls. "I don't know if I want your mouth or your pussy first." Those words on his lips…I don't think I need him to touch me. All he needs to do is whisper everything he wants to do to me in his gravelly voice, and I might just explode on the spot.

"First, my mouth." I punctuate my reply with a light suck to the head of his cock, tasting his pre-cum. Devon lets out a hiss, which turns into a moan when I lower my mouth onto him completely. In one quick movement, he pushes my head down.

His cock is on the larger side, my jaw opening wide at the intrusion. I let out a loud gag and lift my head off him.

Trying again, I hold my breath and suck him. I just gag when I try to breathe, so I keep holding my breath. I continue with my unconventional method of depriving myself of oxygen for the sake of giving Devon the best head of his life.

"Breathe out through your nose," he grunts.

"I know, I just don't want to," I reply, enjoying the constriction and dizziness that I feel each time my head throbs, desperate for oxygen.

"Vi—" Devon is interrupted by his own guttural moan. The next time I cover him with my mouth, he holds me there. I let out a strained moan and feel my core ache. My body loves this roughness. I scratch my nails over his legs as I choke on him, reciprocating his aggressiveness. He responds by tensing his thighs, the muscles rippling under my fingers.

This is so fucking hot.

"Love it when you choke on me, Sweetness." I exhale a long breath from my nose. Devon holds my head still as he thrusts between my lips, his cock knocking on the back of my throat. He moves slowly at first, and then he's relentless as he fucks my mouth.

With a flick of his wrist, his hand seizes my hair and fists it into what feels like a tight ponytail. Saliva drips down my chin, my face aching. I don't stop sucking. I use my hands to fondle his balls, running my finger up the seam in the center until it reaches the base of his cock.

"Violet," he grits. Devon's hand flexes in my hair as if he's restraining himself, his tightening hold causing my scalp to burn. A deep whimper emits from his mouth, and I squeeze my thighs together. I imagine his head tipped back, throat working as he moans my name.

Erotic, wet noises emanate from where we are joined together, and I hold my breath. I suck until my vision blurs from the lack of oxygen again—the breath play is taking me to new heights of arousal.

I pull off him and suck in air, then lean forward to take him in my mouth again until his legs shake.

"Fuck!" he bellows and rips me off him. He stands quickly, and I fall back onto my ass. I'm not on the floor for long because I suddenly feel his hands on me as he picks me up and places me on what feels like a soft bed.

"If I cum, it's going to be inside of you," he pants, his hands skating up my legs. I feel him reach for my jeans, and I help him pull them off.

In just my panties, he rubs a finger over my center. It causes me to lift my hips and allow Devon to slip the lace material off. He shoves two fingers inside of me—I'm so wet that they slide in effortlessly.

"Ready for me, aren't you?" I nod, though he can't see me.

He replaces his fingers with something large that rubs against my entrance. I can only assume it's his cock. I stiffen slightly, and Devon must notice because he pauses too.

"We don't have to do this—" he starts.

"I want this," I whisper. "I'm just nervous, I don't want it to be bad."

Sex with my ex wasn't mind-blowing by any means, so what's to say Devon would be better if my long-term boyfriend wasn't? I nibble at my lip, not out of fear, but out of concern. All this build-up for it to not be amazing has premature disappointment festering in my stomach.

"Do you know how much I want you? There is no alternate universe where it wouldn't be good. I can promise you that, Sweetness." This man is crazy. I squeeze his shoulders in response, and he pushes his tip inside of me. "If you don't want to do this here, we don't have to." He languidly thrusts in and out with just the end of his length.

"I want it here," I grit through my teeth, trying to force my words out over the pleasure that washes over me. He's not even fucking me properly yet. How can he ask me that when teasing me? I let out a rough breath through my nose, and he pulls his cock away from my entrance.

"I'll make this perfect for you."

With those words, he impales me in a motion that's gentle yet firm. I release a loud moan, and he cuts me off by clamping his hand over my mouth. Instead of stopping and letting me get used to his size, he thrusts in and out at a steady pace. He glides into me painlessly, helping me adjust to his size.

"Wouldn't want someone to come and investigate the scream, would we?" he grunts, hand tightening over my mouth. I completely forgot we were in a bedroom at a party, another place someone could easily walk in. I clench around Devon at the thought of being caught. He must feel me tighten around him because he drops forward, his forehead touching mine.

"You like the sound of that? You like the thought of someone walking in and seeing us like this? My dirty fucking Violet." I don't respond and instead, anchor my nails into his back.

He yanks the neckline of my top down so my breasts are freed. The way Devon sucks and worships them makes me feel like a goddess, it's like he can't get enough of me.

He takes full advantage of covering every inch of my chest in wet kisses, the rough surface of his tongue causing delicious friction over my nipples.

"Devon," I breathe. I take his wrist and guide it to my throat, his hand slithers around my neck in a gentle choke. Pleasure blankets itself over me. Each rock of his hips causes an intermittent burst of pleasure to shoot straight to my clit.

"Too slow," I moan, using his words from earlier. He speeds up his pace, but I need more.

I place my hand over his one that's resting on my throat and squeeze, signaling for him to choke me harder.

"You're gonna kill me," he growls and tightens his grip, pumping into me harder. "I can't get enough of you." With his other hand, he places each of my legs over his shoulders and kisses me hard. This angle practically folds me in half. It allows him to hit deeper, causing a louder moan to escape my lips.

After several more thrusts, he slides out of me, and I mewl when he flips me onto my front. He buries my face into the bed, shoving himself inside of me from behind to maintain his rough pounding. The sound of wet slaps and my incoherent, muted babbles bounce around the room as he ruins me.

"So fucking perfect," he groans. I feel so full and clench around him again, a pleasurable sob ripping from my throat. "So good that you're sobbing. You've waited so long for me to fuck you. Next time, I want to see my cum leaking out of you."

My back arches as he lifts my head by my hair. His mouth sits against the side of my face, tongue brushing along my cheekbone as he tastes my tears.

He then reaches under me and rubs my clit, my stomach tightening before I nosedive into my release. An animalistic wail forces itself out of me, and Devon silences me by pushing my face into the bed.

My thighs shake as I thrash around him whilst he still hammers into me. He then freezes momentarily before burying his face into the back of my neck, sluggishly thrusting inside of me until we are nothing but a panting, sweaty mess.

"Christ, Violet," he breathes, resting for several seconds before pulling out of me. I say nothing. My mind is static and my brain is refusing to tune in.

I'm sure if I could see Devon's face, he'd be looking at me with a heated gaze. The only reason I know is because I can feel it. The way he looks at me is so intense that even in the darkest of rooms, his eyes sear every inch of the flesh he's touched, kissed, and sucked.

Devon must be feeling the same as me because he doesn't say a word as we both get dressed to the best of our ability in the pitch-black room. I hear him move toward me, the rough material of my pants grazing my arm when he hands them over.

"Why is your pant leg wet?" he asks as I put them on—the task more difficult than it should be in the dark.

"Some asshole bumped into a guy that I was talking to earlier, it knocked his drink on me."

"What an asshole," Devon drawls. Based on his tone, I have a feeling that he seems satisfied about Vince spilling his drink.

I begin to leave, stopping when I reach the door. I realize I can just turn on the light. My hand finds the switch and hovers over it.

"Violet," Devon calls. "I'll see you at work." I pull my hand away, choosing to leave the room as it was when I entered—dark.

Without looking back, I run straight into the nearest bathroom and try and make myself look like I haven't almost been choked and fucked to death. When I think I look okay,

I head downstairs to find Freya.

I pass dancing bodies and couples who look as if they're about to engage in activities like Devon and I just have. I finally spot Freya in the foyer, only she seems to be arguing with Micah. Her body is tense with her finger pointing at him, but she appears…sad?

Micah reaches out with a comforting touch and pulls her into a friendly embrace. I hover a short distance away, unsure whether to approach. Micah looks up and spots me. He leans down to whisper something in Freya's ear and she turns. Following his gaze, she gives me a weak smile before walking toward me.

"I want to go home," she whispers, and I nod.

"Me too," I agree. I'm more than ready to throw myself into my bed. Micah escorts us outside, and the loud bass booming from a car coming down the street makes my bones vibrate.

It's a sports car that pulls up, and four people hop out. The guy in the passenger seat is oddly familiar…Isaac. I smile when I spot him wearing a huge bandage over his nose, only to feel a little disappointed when I realize that Mari isn't here. Micah angrily storms up to the car.

"Get the fuck off my property. If you're planning on selling shit, go somewhere else," he says to the tall, lean guy getting out of the driver's seat.

"Ah, come on, we're all adults here. I thought we were past the high school stuff." The slim guy opens his arms wide in mock friendliness.

"Shut the fuck up, Connor. Several people here, including myself, have a problem with you and your fucking group. Shit's different now," Micah snarls.

"No shit," Isaac hisses, his gaze unwavering as he looks directly at me.

"Leave my house right fucking now," Micah threatens. Two people in the group look at Connor for their next command, except for Isaac, who is still glaring at me.

"Fine, I just wanted to see you, old friend," Connor says, smirking. "But we'll leave if it'll stop you from getting your panties in a twist." His group kisses their teeth. Dirty looks are thrown at Micah, some at Freya too. "Oh, and Micah, just because you're some LA big shot now, it doesn't mean the past can't come back to haunt you." This Connor guy appears to have no effect on Micah, his threats falling on deaf ears.

I look at Freya who is still uncharacteristically quiet and observing the interaction. Her face has paled, eyes following Micah closely as he watches Connor and Isaac drive off with their friends.

Once the sports car is nothing but distant headlights, Micah shakes his head and walks up to us with his attention mainly on Freya.

"We will keep in touch this time, alright Frey? I fly back to LA next week, and I want to see you before I leave." His voice is gentle compared to the tone he used to tell Connor to leave. Freya nods and smiles softly at him, her keys jingling as she takes them out of her purse. She seems instantly happier now that Connor's posse has gone.

Micah makes sure we get into the car safely and watches us drive off. Though, as we exit the driveway, I can feel another pair of eyes on me.

"What was that about?" I question several minutes into our drive home. Freya's turn signal clicks for a few beats before she answers.

"Connor and Micah have some history. Micah isn't part of that life now, though. Connor also caused some trouble for me when I was eighteen."

"Seems like nobody is a fan of that crew. I know a couple of people who don't get on with Isaac." I'm speaking in relation to Devon and Mari.

"Vi, how the fuck do you know people who don't get on with them?" Freya releases a laugh, the information obviously catching her off guard.

"I'm not a loser, okay? He got into a fight with one of my friends for no reason. He's just a terrible person. He also treats his girlfriend like trash."

"I never thought you were a loser! I'm trying so hard not to ask how you ended up knowing these people, but damn. His girlfriend is that sweet girl who usually wears super long braids." I nod.

"Yeah, Mari."

"They're still together? I saw them at a few parties in high school. Isaac is well known in the area." I don't know what

Freya means by that, but judging by her tone, Isaac being known doesn't sound too positive.

"Small world," I mumble.

"Small world, indeed," Freya agrees as we continue to drive back home in silence.

"You okay though Freya? Seriously," I say after several minutes. I'm worried about her. I don't know what was going on between her and Micah.

"Yeah, I'm good Vi, just some bad memories that came back. You disappeared for a bit at the party, are *you* okay?" She gives a small smile and circles her face with her pointer finger. I flash her a look of confusion and pull down the sun visor above the passenger seat.

My reflection in the mirror shows some makeup that's smudged around my eyes, and my lipstick touch-up has done nothing to hide the stains around my mouth.

Despite my best efforts to clean up in the bathroom, my makeup is mostly worn off. I smash my lips together to conceal my own smile and turn to Freya.

"More than good, Frey," I say. She squeals, my words causing her to do a small jig in her seat. I give a quick thanks to her for giving me a ride and head inside, trying to avoid starting a conversation about what I got up to at the party. When I unlock the front door, I spot Ash knocked out on the couch. I toss a blanket over him before heading upstairs, exhausted and feeling nothing but the dull ache of Devon inside of me.

Chapter 9

Violet

"I don't understand why we have to go shopping," Ash moans as I peruse the rails of the thrift store. He loiters behind me with his skateboard, his horribly bleached hair hanging in front of his eyes.

"You needed a ride, and that ride means we pass the thrift stores," I explain, hovering over a cute skirt. I'm dropping Ash off to go skating with friends. As usual, we stop off to shop.

"Well, it fucking stinks in here," he says, checking out some basketball shorts. I flash him a warning glare at his choice of words. He's right, though. It does smell a little musty, as most thrift stores do. The stench does little to deter me from looking at the clothes, and I continue flicking through them. Ash, on the other hand, lets out a dramatic sigh.

My brother doesn't hate thrifting. I know this because a good portion of his wardrobe contains clothes from second-hand stores.

He does, however, hate going thrifting when it's somewhat against his free will—I guess shopping with me falls into that category.

"Can we at least get food? I want a fat burger." I side-eye him a little because I swear I witnessed him devouring half the contents of our refrigerator before we left.

"You eat like a beast, Ash. Didn't you get food before we left?" I brush him off. He can eat after I pick him up from hanging out with his friends. Ash narrows his eyes at me and flicks his hair out of his face, scoffing loudly.

"Of course I ate before I left, but I'm hungry again. I'm a growing boy and you're depriving me of sustenance."

"I'm depriving you? You've cleaned out the refrigerator. What about *my* sustenance?" I argue. I'm sure we've bickered over this exact same topic earlier this week.

Ash then playfully smacks a mannequin and earns a glare from the older woman behind the cash register. I spot another woman's head shoot up from behind a clothing rail at the sound of the smack. I recognize her.

"Mari?" I ask, excitedly. She looks confused for a second, her brown eyebrows furrowed before raising with recognition.

"Violet! Oh my gosh!" Her face lights up, and she walks around a clothing rack to face me. "Long time no see, how have you been?" Mari wears a green beret over her hair, it's cute and matches her overalls and loafers.

"I'm good, I haven't seen you since the race! Are you okay? What happened?" I ask, my questions coming out at rapid fire.

"I'm okay…" she trails off, avoiding my eyes for a moment. "Isaac and I aren't on great terms, so I haven't been to any more races," she says solemnly. "Sorry about him by the way, he was a little upset."

"Upset? Your boyfriend went crazy. I also saw how he treated you after the fight."

One thing about discussing a friend's relationship is that it's hard not to cross a boundary when you really hate the person they're with. I barely know Isaac or Mari, but I've seen enough to know that Isaac is a complete and utter asshole from the ten minutes I've spent in his presence.

"Yeah, he just gets like that when he loses sometimes. We're having a break right now, so you don't need to worry."

A break? I give Mari a concerned look and she averts her gaze. Ash coughs loudly and shoves me a little when he moves to stand in front of me.

"Hi Mari, I couldn't help but overhear your little conversation with my sister here." He slaps his hand on my shoulder like we're best buddies. "I'm Ash. Ashton Lee, brother to Violet Lee. I apologize for my sister's failure to introduce us. I don't know who this Isaac guy is, but if you need a real man, I'm available." Ash winks flirtatiously, and I shove him away from her. Mari lets out a musical laugh and shakes her head at my brother.

"Ignore him. Ash, go outside for a second whilst I speak to Mari," I say, shooing him toward the store exit.

"Dogs are treated better than me," he mumbles and says something under his breath about me buying him food as he strolls out of the store. The worker looks relieved when he leaves.

"Well, why don't we exchange numbers, and we can hang out at some point?" Mari asks enthusiastically. "I should've asked when we met, but you know, things were a little rushed." *That's one way to describe the night of the race.*

"Sure, we can go for coffee now if you're free? I *really* want to catch up. I just need to drop my brother off somewhere, but I can be back here in fifteen," I suggest, hoping to get to know her more. Mari is nice, she was so welcoming to me at the race. It would be silly not to become closer friends, regardless of the conflict between Devon and Isaac.

"That'd be amazing, Violet," she replies, her voice warm. "I'll get us a table." I go outside to look for Ash, locating him like a bat by following the sound of rolling skateboard wheels. When I find him, he's attempting tricks in the courtyard area of the mall.

"Ash!" I call, noticing a security guard eyeing him with

displeasure. "Are you ready to go?" I dangle my keys.

"Finally," he huffs, kicking up his skateboard and making a beeline for the parking lot.

I drive him a couple of miles to the skatepark, instantly noticing his group of friends. They're all dressed similarly in spray-painted pants that they've designed themselves. Ash is about to close the car door, but I lean across and stop him.

"Ash, I'll pick you up in a few hours, okay? If you mess me around with picking you up again, you can get the bus."

The last time I dropped him off, I returned to pick him up at the time we agreed on. He made me wait an hour by sending me texts claiming he was *'almost there'*. When he did arrive, he handed me a cold, half-eaten burger as a peacemaker. Peace was not made.

"Yeah, sure. Love ya." He blows several air kisses in succession at me, slams the door shut, and then hops on his skateboard to join his friends.

I text Mari asking if she still wants to hang, and she says that she's got a table for us in the cafe next to the thrift store. I rush back to find her sipping tea and reading something as I pay for my drink.

"Younger brothers are exhausting," I sigh and drop into the chair opposite, which causes her to slam the book closed.

"He's funny." Mari smiles, tucking her book into her tote bag. I can't help but notice the shirtless man on the cover and suppress a smile as she continues talking. "I wish I had a sibling. I only have cousins...*lots of them*."

"It's fun, but we argue a bunch. I think he's just at that age. My parents are pilots and are out of the country most of the time. They work odd schedules," I explain. "It's why Ash and I are so close and why I'm his chauffeur." Mari snorts a little at my sarcasm.

"I'd rather be giving a younger sibling a ride than my drunk boyfriend at three a.m.," she says, obviously referring to Isaac.

"Thank god you didn't have to pick him up from the party yesterday."

"Party?" she asks, confused. *Oh no.* Does she know that Isaac was trying to get into a party?

"Yeah, I saw Isaac with a group of friends. I didn't see you, were you there?" I ask, taking a sip of my drink.

"Oh, that's why he wasn't home this weekend," she replies, completely unfazed. "And no, I was at home. I haven't been to a party in forever."

"Yeah, he got turned away as soon as he arrived. Some guy called Connor was driving." Mari scrunches her nose and nods, familiar with the name.

"I'm glad they got turned away, I can't stand his friends," she huffs. She's happy her boyfriend and his friends were refused entry to a party?

"Wait, why don't you like them?" I'm probably crossing a boundary by asking. It's none of my business.

"They're bad people. All of them are involved in criminal activities. Isaac has his moments too, but he just does racing

123

now."

"Then why are you with him?" I ask, a little too intrusively. *Tone it down, Violet.*

"Financial struggles. Moved in together when we were young, and I can't afford to move out. We're kind of broken up right now anyways, remember?" True, she did say they were on a break earlier.

It must suck to live with someone you've split up with. Especially with someone like Isaac.

"If you need somewhere to stay in the meantime, feel free to let me know. You can stay at mine," I offer. She declines, shaking her head.

"I'll be fine. Thanks though, Violet." I leave the conversation there. I'm tempted to rant about how awful Isaac was at the race and decide to keep my opinions to myself instead. I'd also be a complete hypocrite.

Devon's no angel, and she probably knows that.

Mari gets up to order some more tea before we fall into a conversation about ourselves. It turns out that she wants to be a sports photographer, which is why she was photographing the race—she's building up her portfolio.

"Oh, I have access to a local art studio if you want to share the space?" she asks. Excitement flares up in me, studio space would be a complete dream. "I work at one part-time, so it would be nice to go halves on space if you're interested?"

"Are you serious?" I can't believe this. What are the chances that the one girl I befriended at a race is willing to share studio space? *Maybe I should get out more.*

"Yes! Nobody uses it on weekends because it's closed. I have a spare key. Just make sure you don't leave it wrecked so that Monday classes can take place."

"Are you sure I won't get into trouble?" I ask cautiously. "Also, how can you trust me?" I know Mari is kind, but she barely knows me.

"You won't get into trouble because I'm a loyal employee. Also, I'm pretty confident that I can trust you. You stood up for me at the race, and you just offered me a place to stay." I have no choice but to take her word for it. We sip and chat until the dreaded conversation comes up: Devon.

"So…Devon Blackstone, hm?" Mari perks up and I smile awkwardly. *Devon Blackstone.* His full name.

At this point, Mari probably knows more about him than me considering they go to the same races. Devon also made it seem like they went to the same school when he mentioned her the other night.

"What about Devon Blackstone?" I experiment with his name on my tongue. I don't know if names can be considered attractive. If there's a list, the name Devon Blackstone would be up there.

"Are you two…you know? Dating? You said you weren't when we last spoke, so I'm curious if things have developed." Mari's smile is a blend of anticipation and excitement. Developed. Sure, if we're being modest.

"I don't know what we are, actually," I answer truthfully.

There's a subdued pang in my chest. Whilst I told Mari about Devon and I not being together at the race, the events that have transpired since make the words taste bitter in my mouth.

I know that I wish there was something more than whatever friendship limbo we're in now.

"Fine, fine," she yields, peering over the rim of her mug. She looks a little shifty, like she's unsure of my reaction to her words. "It was kind of attractive when he walked through the crowd to reach you at the race...and the way you stayed back like you knew he was going to come and get you." She rests a hand over her heart and visibly swoons.

I take a deep breath, feeling a knot of anxiety in my stomach.

"Yeah, I guess it was kind of attractive." I try to keep my voice light and unbothered.

Mari raises a thick eyebrow. "Just kind of?" It feels like she's chiseling away at my lies, or at the very least, knows that I am lying.

My face heats a little and I tear at a napkin on the table. "Yes, just kind of. But I don't think it means anything, you know?"

"No, I don't know. All I know is that you've got one of the hottest guys ever wrapped around your finger, and you're sitting here acting oblivious. Either that, or you're in denial about your feelings for him. If you like him and he likes you, what is this weird uncertainty?" Mari flaps her hands in exasperated confusion.

One of the hottest guys ever? *Oh my god.*

I really hope Mari and I's definition of hot is somewhat similar. It's physically paining me to not just search him online now that I know his entire name.

"Violet?" Mari asks, drawing me out of my thoughts. I completely forgot to respond to her question, and she looks a little concerned.

"You're right, it's just a little complicated." If only she knew that Devon Blackstone is faceless to me. A biking enigma. Mari's words make sense, but Devon's hidden identity and my back and forth in wanting to see his face is enough to keep us in a constant teasing state. Mari nods silently and focuses on pouring herself another cup of tea.

This discussion about Devon rekindles my burning desire to know as much as I can about him without seeing his face. I'm admittedly getting more impatient now, especially since I've slept with him.

I watch Mari add a packet of sugar to her drink and bounce my leg under the table. I try to restrain myself from asking her about Devon, afraid that revealing how little I know about him will be embarrassing.

Each passing second feels like an eternity as I withhold the need to satisfy my curiosity. I'm going to approach this calmly, no need to rush into it.

"How much money does a winner get from racing, anyway?" I ask. Devon mentioned it when I asked what he

127

did for work, so I'm interested to know how much he earns.

"I don't really know, but it's a lot. One time, when Devon didn't race, Isaac won and got around five thousand," Mari explains. "I think the betting pool is huge for these races, and the way it's organized means the winner gets a large payout. People who don't attend also place bets."

"Damn." I don't know how much mechanics earn, but with Devon's need to constantly overpay me at work, I'm sure he's living comfortably with all of that income combined.

"Exactly. Your man always wins, so it's easy money for him."

I make a face at Mari referring to him as my man, and she looks at me apologetically. Although he's not yet mine, I can feel myself burning up as we talk about him.

"What do you know about Devon?" I ask as casually as possible, sipping my drink. The hot liquid only makes me warmer, and I shrug off my cardigan before I start to sweat.

"Um…" Mari's glossy, brown pencil-lined lips press together. She looks at me with a baffled expression. "I think you know more about Devon than me." I lean forward out of impatience, causing the table to rattle slightly. Mari looks at me with panicked doe eyes.

"Mari, I promise I was telling you the truth when I said that I don't know what we are. It's more of a…" How do I even describe this? Dating? A talking stage? A blind date?

"We are in a situationship."

If I thought that made things clearer, Mari looks ten times

more confused.

"What is a situationship?" she asks.

Fuck it. I've been *dying* to tell someone about this.

"Forget what I just said, here's the thing…"

I explain everything to Mari. By everything, I mean all except the X-rated details. From the first time he filled up his bike, all the way to seeing him at the party.

By the time I finish speaking, Mari takes a huge gulp of tea and sets it down calmly. She takes a slow breath in and releases it along with a string of questions.

"You have never seen his face?! How did you only just find out his name at the race? Wait, so you don't even know if he's *hot*?" Some very good questions to which I have no reasonable answer for.

"I don't know, it just kind of happened. The whole anonymous thing was fun and we just…continued, I guess." Mari looks at me in complete shock, her dark eyes wide and incredulous.

"I don't even know what to say." She thinks for a moment before letting out a loud gasp. "Do you have a mask kink?" I choke on my tea, not expecting those words to come from her mouth.

"No!" I sputter. Though, she might be right.

"Hmm." Mari ponders over my words. "Whatever floats your boat. The only question I have is *when* do you actually plan on seeing his face?"

"I don't know. There have been times when I could've, but

I just chose not to."

"All he has to do is take off his helmet…or mask, or whatever. This could've been done in the first meeting, how strange." Mari giggles and I laugh along with her. It does sound odd when explaining it out loud. "And it's only been a few weeks. You haven't tried to search for him online or anything?" She looks at me in exasperation.

"No! That'd ruin the reveal. Besides, you only just told me his last name," I admit, winking at her.

"Oh gosh, you didn't even know his last name!" Mari throws her head back in a fit of laughter, her soft chuckles causing a few heads to briefly turn in our direction. "You know, you could've just searched Dynamite Devon. It'd probably just show images of him when he was a kid. You have good self-control, I would've found his extended family by now," she says.

For two hours, Mari and I engage in mindless chatter with the occasional poke at my so-called mask kink. My phone then buzzes with Ash's message, letting me know he's finished skating.

"I wish we could chat for longer, but Ash needs picking up," I say, pouting.

"Same! This was so fun, I'm honestly so excited for you to see Devon's face. I'm not going to say anything about the way he looks, even though I let it slip that he was good-looking earlier." Mari pretends to zip her lips as I shoot her a smile.

I can't help but wonder if I have a thing for masks, Devon, or both. I'm sure it's both.

Suddenly, my feelings of apprehensiveness start to seep back into me.

"Oh, Mari. Before we leave, I want to get some advice," I say, toying with my car keys.

"Sure, what's up?"

"Devon has an amazing personality, and we get on so well. A big factor in our friendship is that he hasn't revealed his face. I know his mask shouldn't make a difference, but I can't help but wonder if things will just fizzle out once this is all over."

"Are you worried you won't be attracted to him?" she asks. "I can assure you that I *doubt* that'd be a problem."

"No, it's not that…it's because this anonymity plays such an important part between us. I dunno, what would you do in my position?"

"Oh, I see." Mari ponders over my words for a moment, placing her tote bag on her shoulder as she stands up. "You're overthinking it and approaching this way too pessimistically. I mean, why don't you just ask him to show you his face next time you see him? The whole mask thing seems fun, but maybe as time goes on, you're both realizing that the mask is becoming pointless. Communicate with him, Vi."

She's so right.

"You're a genius," I say, holding the cafe door open for her.

"You could've totally come to that conclusion yourself." She laughs softly as we approach my car. "I think you just wanted someone to validate your choices."

"Probably. I also just needed a verbal slap in the face to relax."

"Well, that's what friends are for, right? One of us spirals about something minor, and the other makes them see sense. Or I could just feed into your delusions." I let out a sharp laugh.

"Thanks Mari, seriously. It feels pretty good to talk to someone about this."

"I can imagine how relieving it must feel to admit that you have a mask kink," she jokes, and I twist my lips in amusement.

"If you don't drop the mask kink thing, I might conveniently forget to text you when the big reveal happens," I say to her, unlocking my car.

"This has gotta be blackmail. You know I'll be waiting for your text regardless."

"We'll see," I joke, shutting the car door and rolling down the window. "You need a ride?" Mari shakes her head, hitching the strap of her bag higher onto her shoulder.

"I'm good, thanks. I was just seeing you off. I need to do some more errands anyway." With that, we quickly say our goodbyes, and I watch Mari enter another store before heading to the skatepark.

Now, there's only one way I'll approach Devon the next

time I see him: I'm going to ask him to take off the mask.

Chapter 10

Devon

"I need to see your face," Violet says the moment I step into the gas station. She's busy slicing open the bulk packaging of some drinks that need to be stocked and jots down numbers on a sheet of paper.

"Hello to you too," I greet, a little surprised by her eagerness.

"So?" she asks impatiently, her brown eyes peering up at me. My steps slow as I approach her.

We haven't spoken since the party. My ego swells with the assumption that I made her feel so good, she wants nothing more than to finally see my face.

"I have a question," I announce to her.

"What? You didn't even respond to me properly." Violet

scrunches her face and her frustration shows through her tone.

"Was it perfect for you?" Violet's eyes suddenly widen as she remembers what I said at the party.

"You're talking about the sex?"

"Yes, Violet. I'm talking about when you choked on my cock and came around it at the party." Violet swallows uncomfortably.

"Yes. It was...good," she grinds out as if I'm forcing her to speak. Her hand tightens around the pen knife that she's using to unpack the drinks. I wouldn't put it past her to throw it at me if I continue to tease her—it's a risk that I'm willing to take.

"Good? I think it was more than good because now you want to *desperately* see my face." The confidence she showed when I first walked in has withered away, replaced by a flustered state that's reminiscent of when we first met. I notice her chest rise and fall with more intensity, mine doing the same. "If you really want to see my face, you need to beg for it."

As usual, I take off my jacket and gloves, my eyes never leaving Violet's. She stares at my hands, which grip the bottom of the mask.

"Please let me see your face." *Fuck.* I was planning on just teasing her, but her sweet begs threaten to weaken my resolve.

"Beg more, *Sweetness.*" Her pink lips part and she nods

again, hanging onto my every word.

"I want to see your face, Devon. Please," she pleads. Her eyes are still fixed on where my hands rest on the mask.

I swallow, my throat suddenly dry. "No."

She reels back like she's been ripped away from my spell, and my fingers twitch at the temptation of removing the black fabric.

"What, why?" she demands, her voice tinged with irritation.

"I have something planned." I'm lying. I just don't want her to see my face for the first time in a rundown gas station. I want it to be more romantic. I also want to be groomed; my hair is now growing back, and it needs shaping up immediately.

"What? So, when will I see it?" Her voice raises slightly. I can tell she's humiliated and embarrassed that she begged for no reason.

"Soon," I say and open up my backpack, retrieving a cardboard food box. I slam it on the counter in front of her. "Open it. You'll forgive me once you see what's inside." Well, I think she'll forgive me.

Violet reaches under the plastic barrier and snatches the box, her actions rough with annoyance. When she opens it, she looks at me suspiciously. Joy crosses her face when she realizes that I'm not playing with her.

"Devon…" She peeks inside the box again. "You actually brought me Baklava?" Her reaction to my small gift almost has me reaching for my phone so I can call Kas and ask him to make ten more batches. She pulls out a slice and bites into it, moaning.

"Fuck," she breathes. I find myself staring at her the same way she looked at me when I was about to take off my ski mask.

"I don't think you know what those noises do to me," I grit, my eyes unmoving from her mouth.

"I know what they do to you," she flirts. *This girl.*

"Now that I think about it, I've changed my answer."

"Answer to what?" Violet places the uneaten half of the Baklava slice back into the box and dusts her hands together.

"That time when you were asking me questions about myself. My favorite thing to eat isn't Baklava, it's you," I say, stepping closer to the counter that separates us.

"That's cute." She shrugs and flicks her hair over her shoulder, practically shutting me down. It bothers me and she knows it. A smile dances on her lips as she picks up her pencil and goes back to numbering stock.

"Are you teasing me?" Anger and arousal swirl through me, and I'm contemplating throwing myself through the plastic partition.

"Teasing you? Teasing would be someone saying they'd remove their mask if I begged and then not doing it." She's definitely teasing.

"Yeah, that does sound like teasing, whoever did that must be an asshole." I decide to walk slowly around the counter instead of destroying the plastic that separates us. "How could you ever forgive someone like that?" I ask mockingly. My arms cage her against the counter, and her hand fists tightly around her pencil as I press myself flush against her back. "Nervous or turned on, Violet?" I whisper.

"What if a customer sees us in this position?" She looks over her shoulder at me. It's early in the morning and the sun has risen. That means more customers are likely to come in.

Just to be safe, I turn on the radio that's behind me and increase the volume.

"Don't start backing up now, Sweetness. If you're worried

about people seeing us, then I'll have to make this quick." I skim my hand up her spine and down again, rubbing her back soothingly. Then, I slide down the length of her body and lift her long skirt. Perfect attire for what I'm about to do.

"Dev—"

"Bend over, Violet."

A shiver wracks her body, and she bends over, her chest resting on the counter. I lean forward to smell her musky arousal through her panties. Dampness seeps through as I rub my finger over her clit.

"Remember, we're at a gas station—not a forest, or a loud party where nobody can hear your moans and whimpers. I suggest you try and keep quiet…if you can. The radio is no match against your screams," I remind her.

Her body relaxes as she releases a large lungful of air, only to tense up again when I trail my hands down her toned thighs to her calves. My hands rise back up to her hips so I can peel away the thin barrier of fabric that hides the one thing I've been wanting to taste.

I insert a finger inside of her, and she shuffles from one foot to the other like she's trying to either get used to the feeling or wants more. Fucking her slowly with my digit causes her hips to rock against my hand.

When she steps back to try and get me to move faster and deeper, I slap her ass. Hard. I love that she knows what she wants from me, but I love teasing her more.

"Stay still," I growl. Violet ignores me and continues to

move restlessly. Her fidgeting causes her skirt to flutter down from where I pushed it up and out of the way. "If you don't do as I say, I swear to god I will make you scream in front of your customers," I lie. That makes her stop.

From this angle, it's difficult for me to try and lick her center from behind—the counter is tall, and she's not as bent over as I would like. I reposition myself between her and the counter, pulling up my ski mask so her pussy is directly in front of my face.

Now enveloped by the soft, flowing fabric of her skirt, I grab her thighs and pull her into my face. I instantly latch onto her clit, her legs buckling. I give a firm tap to the back of both knees, and her legs weaken further—it causes her to practically sit on my face, succumbing to the mercy of my mouth.

"Oh my god," she whispers.

God? Not quite.

Her throaty speech only makes me grip her ass and suck harder. I want to feel her arousal seeping down my chin in an uncontrollable stream, just like it did when I devoured her on my bike. I know that she's turned on, but I want proof.

Slick, wet proof.

I hold her still with one hand, using my other to finger her. My tongue worms out to lick around her hole, and she spreads her legs even wider.

"Devon," she mumbles, her thighs trembling against my ears.

"Watching you lose control is almost as hot as watching you try and gain it," I say into her flesh. She reaches down and feels around the shelves under the counter until she finds my head.

Suddenly, the bell on the door rings loudly. We both freeze. I don't doubt that my earlier threat is running through her head. If a customer comes to pay, it would be impossible for them to see me unless they stood behind the counter. It wouldn't be impossible for them to see or hear Violet orgasm, though.

I expect her to pull away, kick me, stomp on me—anything to prevent me from feasting on her. She does nothing of the sort and instead, grips my head harder. The burning encourages me to maintain my painfully slow pace. With Violet's hips rolling against my face in desperate urgency, I realize that she's trying to speed things up.

She doesn't want to stop.

She wants to cum.

Good girl.

Violet is getting tongue fucked into oblivion behind the cash register while a customer shops.

The risk of being caught probably adds to the pleasure, and I swipe my finger over a more forbidden hole on her body. She flinches hard and knocks over something on the counter.

"Shit," she hisses. I'm assuming the customer is still browsing because I have yet to detect their approach.

"More, quickly," Violet whimpers quietly. I can imagine

her gripping the counter for dear life in both fear and pleasure.

My dick throbs, and I remove one hand from Violet's ass so I can touch myself. I unzip my pants and pull out my cock, groaning as I fist it. I'm so turned on, that after a few pumps I can feel myself on the edge already. I'm not one to cum so soon and Violet is seriously testing me.

I unhand myself, holding off on my own release to give my full attention to Violet.

Her thighs quiver violently as I lash at her with my tongue. She keels over at the waist, unable to support her own weight. I pull my mouth away so I can insert two fingers inside of her and talk her toward her orgasm in hushed whispers.

"Watch the customer on the cameras and tap my head when they're coming, okay?" With most of her weight resting on my shoulders, her entire body moves when she nods her head.

"Don't be scared of letting go, Violet. You know I'd never let someone else witness you breaking apart for me." I kiss her clit, suck it lightly and then pull away.

"We just have to time it right. Do you think we can do that, Sweetness?" Her body moves again with the movement of her head, and I do the same kiss and suck to her center again.

"Can you see how your hips jerk faster when you're close?" I ask, speeding up my fingers. Her reaction stays true to my words, paired with muted pants. "And then they rock when you're not so close." I slow my fingers down, and her hips move accordingly. "See?" I alternate between rapid motions and a leisurely tempo.

Regardless of the speed of my fingers, I make sure to massage them against her internal walls each time they are thoroughly inside of her.

"He's coming…I'm coming." She speaks in breathless pants. So quiet, that I almost miss her words.

I take that as my cue to stop playing around and fucking devour her. Uncaring if I can breathe or not, I pull her further into my face.

The sudden feel of my tongue against her takes her straight to an orgasm so intense, it catches me by surprise.

"Devon!" she grunts almost soundlessly, just as I hear the sound of a refrigerator closing. I don't stop until I've licked my way through every single wave that rocks her body. As she comes down from her high, I hear footsteps approaching. Violet stands up immediately.

"Just this, please," a male voice says.

"No problem," Violet responds, impressively calm after just exploding on my face. "Four-eighty."

"Do you take card payments?"

She clears her throat before speaking again. "Of course."

I hear the beep of a card machine and retreating footsteps a few seconds later. The bell sounds to signal his departure, and I take it as my sign to get up. I'm not done yet. I want my release too.

I slide out from underneath Violet and stand behind her as

she slumps over the counter, her forehead resting on the surface.

I hold her down by the nape of her neck and flip her skirt onto her back. A quiet moan releases itself from her throat.

Gripping my dick, I continue where I left off. It doesn't take me long to cum with this view of her bare ass. On the final pump of my hand, my release surges out of the head of my cock.

I watch as it trickles down from her ass cheeks onto her thighs. She gasps at the sensation and her head begins to lift. I quickly pull down the bottom of my ski mask, noticing the absurdity of me choosing to cover my face first and my exposed cock second.

She gapes at me, desire clouding her eyes as she watches me pat down her skirt over my mess. I then grab my helmet and storm toward the gas station exit, leaving her drenched in my cum just as a car pulls into the lot.

"Oh," I call when I reach the door. "Don't even think about wiping that off until you finish your shift."

"What—"

"See you soon, Sweetness." Her mouth opens and closes, completely bewildered. I hold the door open for a customer who smiles at me politely, oblivious to what Violet and I are talking about.

Each step toward my bike feels mechanical, and turning on the engine seems to be the equivalent of being doused with a bucket of cold water. It washes me with the realization that I can't keep playing this anonymous character anymore.

What was meant to be fun at first, has now turned tortuous. I now feel like I owe it to Violet to show my face after doing that to her.

I'm sure that nobody in their right mind goes from gifting the girl they're obsessed with, to jerking off all over her backside in the span of several minutes.

Yeah, I'm not seeing her until I'm in an acceptable state of mind.

I don't think taking the mask off will make a difference in how much we like each other. It's so obvious that we view each other as more than friends. It seems stupid to carry this on.

Making my way home, I brainstorm all the possible ways I can execute the grand reveal. Maybe a cute picnic date or a nice meal out?

No…it all seems so lackluster.

My brain is wracking with ideas all the way home. I notice Micah's car outside when I pull up to the house. Micah's a great guy. He's outgoing, loud, and intense. Unfortunately, that isn't the type of energy I need right now when I have plans to make regarding my face.

"Dev, you coming to brunch tomorrow?" Micah booms the second I step into the house. He's stuffing his face with eggs as Kas hunches over the stove cooking breakfast. "A get-together before I fly back out," he adds.

"Yeah, sure," I say, my answer blunter than intended with

the exhaustion from my lack of sleep starting to hit. The only thing keeping me awake right now is the smell of Kas' cooking.

"Freya's coming too. You remember that girl that got fucked over by Connor when he tried selling at my party one time?"

"Doesn't ring a bell," I reply, pulling out a chair at the table.

"She's a friend of mine. She had short red hair and was with the hot girl with long black hair at the party the other day." Violet was with a girl with short red hair for most of the party. Now Micah's got my attention.

"Oh, right," I reply in a tight voice, trying not to swing at Micah for calling Violet hot.

"Yeah, Violet is her name…I think. Freya is bringing her to brunch." *Fuck, fuck, fuck.*

Unless I decide not to go to this brunch, Violet will see what I look like. I was thinking that I'd take her out and show my face. Maybe I can catch her off guard now. Kas watches me carefully as he plates up some eggs, turning away when he notices me looking at him.

I know he's onto me because he saw me trailing Violet at the party and nearly blew my cover.

"Message me the details and I'll be there. Kas, can you give me a ride? I don't fancy taking my bike." I always fancy taking my bike, but I don't want Violet spotting it again.

"Alright, I've gotta run. Thanks for breakfast, Kas. Also,

don't mention Connor around Freya," Micah says, standing up and slapping his hand into my palm as he leaves. Kas takes Micah's now vacant seat and passes me a plate of food, leaving us to eat breakfast together.

I watch Kas gobble up several mouthfuls of egg—the guy must eat at least a carton a day. He throws me a few glances between chews. The same glances he's been giving me every day since the party.

"Right, spit it out Kacper," I say, disregarding his nickname and breaking the silence between us. Kas holds up his hand whilst he finishes chewing, then asks his burning question.

"Why was a girl looking for you at the party, and why were you sneaking around her the entire time?" His knife scrapes across his plate and it makes my teeth hurt. The high-pitch noise fills the void of silence in the room as I try to come up with an answer that doesn't make me sound insane.

"I wouldn't call it sneaking," I utter, cutting up my own food.

"She asked me if I had seen you, and you stood behind her flapping your arms at me," Kas grunts, shoveling eggs onto a slice of toast.

"That's because I had to be stealthy, we have an unconventional relationship."

Kas nods hesitantly. "Unconventional…right."

"She's never seen my face," I blurt out in a desperate attempt at trying to justify my actions. Kas stops chewing and looks at me like I'm an idiot.

"Wait, is this who you've been seeing when you go for your night rides?"

"Yep," I chirp. I can't help but smile.

"And she's never seen your face?"

"Never took off my ski mask in front of her." Kas rolls his eyes, but doesn't ask any more questions.

"She will see your face at the brunch. You can't eat with your ski mask on," he says, his speech slowing toward the end as if speaking to a toddler.

"Exactly." Kas shakes his head and releases an amused huff.

"Good luck." Kas is the complete opposite of me when it comes to women. He's almost caveman-like. He fucks women without uttering so much as hello and goodbye.

Within the fight community, it's somewhat of a bet to see what woman will crack his hard exterior. I've known Kas for over ten years, and I've not seen him show an active interest in any person aside from one girlfriend he had for a day in middle school.

Whilst I've only known Violet for a few weeks or so, I'm sure the idea of what's happening between us is completely foreign to Kas. I know that as much as he wants to deny it, a small part of him is excited to see it unfold tomorrow. Even though I've enjoyed this masked business, I'm excited too.

Chapter 11

Violet

Freya has invited me to eat with some of her friends. I guess Micah actually followed up on catching up with her before he flies back to LA. He's decided to invite a bunch of people to a small brunch so that he can say goodbye to everyone at the same time.

As usual, I've dropped my brother off at the skatepark and by doing so, I'm running fifteen minutes late. I quickly shoot Freya a text to let her know that I won't be getting there on time, and she replies almost immediately.

Me: Running late but I think I can make it in 10
Freya: Np! Ordered you the french toast that you like
Freya: That ok?

Me: Ty! Will be there soon :)

"Crap," I sigh, putting my car into drive. I step on the gas and with no traffic, I make it to the diner in exactly ten minutes. I almost forget to shift to park before rushing into the establishment. My eyes scan the tables for a recognizable face, and I immediately spot Freya waving at me.

"Hey! Sorry I'm late," I huff when I reach her. Some of the guys have started eating, whilst others are still waiting for their food. I'm welcomed with several grunts and nods. I recognize a few guys from the party as I get comfortable in my seat at the end of the table.

I chat with Freya for a bit and then briefly acknowledge the guy sitting in front of me with a light smile. A waitress places down two plates of French Toast in front of us.

"Good taste." I smile at his identical plate of food, wiping my utensils with some napkins before using them. His head is down and he doesn't reply whilst he eats. In fact, he doesn't even acknowledge me. A little rude, but whatever. I don't mind because I'm too busy figuring out a way to eat this without making an absolute mess.

"You guys enjoying your food?" Freya asks. It's just me and this dude sitting right at the end of the table, so her question is obviously directed at us.

"It's great," I reply, feeling the sickly syrup run down my throat.

"Mhm, the sweetness is a little overpowering, though." I almost give myself whiplash with the speed at which I lift my head.

Sweetness.

I'd recognize that voice anywhere. I pause with my fork halfway to my mouth and completely scrutinize the guy in front of me until recognition fills my body. He's looking at me, the corner of his mouth tilted up slightly like he's trying not to laugh.

His eyes are identical to Devon's. I could recognize that sharp, green gaze anywhere. Hell, it's all I've seen peering out of the ski mask for weeks.

His lips are full and topped with a defined cupid's bow. They sit under his strong nose, which only reinforces the sharp ridges on his face. Ridges I've mapped with my fingers each time I've had the opportunity to touch him.

He has a small, silver hoop earring that glints in the light. I remember feeling it at the party. The accessory only adds to his striking look, and it's topped off with short, brown hair that's buzzed close to his scalp—it looks like it has been cut recently and suits him perfectly.

Then, he tilts his head and looks at me lazily. That is totally Devon.

He's stunning.

It's taking everything in me not to crawl across the table just to get to him.

"Devon?"

"Violet."

"What the—" I start.

"Oh yeah, sorry. I forgot to introduce you both. You probably met at Micah's party. Violet, this is Devon. Devon, this is Violet," Freya introduces. Met is the biggest understatement of the century. I press my lips together to keep my face neutral.

"Nice to meet you, Violet. We met briefly at the party, I think?" Devon responds. He holds out his hand for me to shake, his eyes sparkling with mischief.

His hand envelops mine. I try to make our handshake quick, but he squeezes my hand when I try to pull away—his grip tightening and holding on just a beat longer than what is considered customary. I struggle to speak. My heart pounds against my ribcage at a tempo so intense, I fear it might either flatline or explode and wipe out the entire diner.

"Hey," I manage to choke out, my voice caught in a hushed exhale.

Freya introduces me to the rest of Micah's friends, and I struggle to remember their names. It dawns on me that Kas is the guy with the huge bruise that I met upstairs at Micah's. He gives me a small nod of recognition.

Trying to compose myself, I take another mouthful of French Toast. I'm purposely avoiding eye contact with Devon; I certainly wasn't prepared for this moment to happen in the middle of a brunch with people around.

The whole situation is absurd, and the fact that I went a month without seeing Devon's face, or knowing his name for half of that time seems ridiculous.

"You look confused," Devon says, speaking up suddenly.

If I hadn't already kissed those lips, I would question whether they even existed. Still in shock and staring at his face, I don't respond.

"It's me, Violet," he reassures. "Ask me questions only I'd know the answers to." He leans back completely unbothered and smiles expectantly at me. He knows that I know it's him. I place my fork onto my plate and lean back in my chair.

"What pump do you always fill up at?" I ask.

"Pump two," he responds immediately.

"What beverage do you buy at the gas station for—"

"Coffee."

"What name did the angry customer call me before he left?" Devon hesitates, his eye twitching.

"No comment."

We exchange a prolonged gaze, the hilarity of the situation sinking in as we stare at each other, trying to hold back our laughter.

I break out into a giggle. Freya halts her conversation with someone next to her to fixate on me as if I am out of my mind. Then, she glances at Devon who is attempting to conceal his laughter by stuffing his face with French Toast.

Everyone at the table remains oblivious to our interaction, except for Kas, who has a smile tugging at his lips. Freya seems puzzled by the exchange, then nods slowly as if confirming something with herself.

"Ohhh, the party," she mouths, nodding excitedly.

Freya thinks that Devon is the same guy I hooked up with at the party and she is correct. I did fool around with Devon *a lot* during the party...and before the party...and after the party, too. I give her a shy smile, and she responds with a wink before diverting her attention to others at the table.

When I shift my gaze back to Devon, he's looking at me with a smug grin. We consume our meals, our eyes meeting frequently as I take bites of my French Toast. There's only a little bit of food left over. I'm too anxious to even attempt to finish it. Devon smiles at me, then clears his throat.

"I'm going for a smoke," he announces. I'm confused for a moment because I thought he had quit smoking. When he stands up, he looks at me and jerks his head toward the back of the diner. Only then do I realize that he is giving me a signal to follow him.

"I'll join you," I state, rising abruptly from my seat.

Freya gives me a strange look because she knows I don't smoke. I tilt my head discreetly toward Devon's back as he strolls through the crowded diner. She nods in understanding, doing her usual excited jig.

Devon's imposing figure is easy to track through the bustling diner crowd. I follow him past the restrooms, then out of a fire exit door where we end up facing each other in silence.

"So..." he begins.

"So..."

"You like what you see?" he teases, reaching out to grab a

strand of my hair.

"Eh," I respond, playfully rolling my eyes. He steps closer and yanks me into a kiss. I savor the feel of my palms on his face, and he squeezes me against him as if we might become one.

I don't know what I was expecting after seeing his face. Maybe a lessened attraction? A horrid realization that I don't like him now that I've seen his face?

What I feel is nothing different. In fact, I feel the exact same as I did when he kissed me every single time prior to this.

Just as explosive, just as exciting, and just as obsessed as I was when I first met him. When we break apart, I study his face in the sunlight. He has small freckles dotted across his nose. Cute.

"You scared the shit out of me, Violet. I thought you weren't going to turn up, you would have foiled my plan," he says as if he was some heinous villain—the way he refers to his face reveal as a plan is enough to make me roar with laughter.

"Did you plan this?" I ask, using my sleeve to dab at my watering eyes. "I'm impressed with the whole *sweetness* thing."

"It's not funny! I was genuinely stressed. I had it partly planned when I found out you were coming to brunch yesterday and decided to see how it would go," he answers, shrugging his shoulders. "I ended up just saying nothing at the table until Freya randomly gave me the perfect opening."

He was stressed out over this. Warmth flourishes in my abdomen at the thought of Devon losing his mind over me seeing his face and trying to plan it out.

"I honestly thought I would go crazy not seeing your face after the party," I admit. "I was about to rip off the mask myself in the gas station after you teased me with it. You literally left me…dirty." When he left the station after releasing all over my ass, I was confused, albeit furiously turned on. I wasn't even mad that he stormed out after because I knew he'd be back. Devon always comes back.

"Sorry about that. I panicked if I'm being honest," he says. He scratches his head, muscles stretching against his tee.

"I didn't wash it off, in case you were wondering," I whisper. Devon tips his head back and groans.

"You're killing me, Violet. What have you done to me?"

"No, what have you done to *me*? I was perfectly okay to let you do things to me without seeing your face. Do you know how crazy that is?" The fire exit door opens suddenly. A chef bumbles out, briefly regarding us as he lights up a cigarette. Devon turns at the sound of the lighter, then quickly looks away from the nicotine-filled stick.

"Crazy to us, but even crazier to other people. Kas thought the mask thing was stupid." Devon smirks. "He saw me trailing you through the whole of Micah's party."

"Mari pretty much said the same thing, she said I have a mask kink." I whisper the last part of my sentence so the chef

156

doesn't hear. Devon bursts out laughing, resting his hand on his chest to calm himself.

"You do," he agrees. I give him a weak glare and look away from him in embarrassment. "When I saved you from that customer, I was like your very own Batman."

"Relax," I snicker, looking toward the chef who is watching us skeptically with his cigarette hanging out of his mouth. "The mask was hot, so don't be offended if I ask you to put it on again in the future."

"I won't," he promises. "But it does make it easier to kiss you now."

"This is the first time we've seen each other outside of, like, ten p.m. to seven a.m. too," I point out.

We really restricted ourselves for the fun of it. I can't help but wonder if the attraction and chemistry would have been the same if Devon had taken off his helmet and ski mask the first time we met.

Devon's words about there being no alternate universe where the sex wouldn't be good comes to mind. I don't think there's an alternate universe where we wouldn't have some sort of chemistry.

"Do you think that we will be the same without the mask? I mean, the whole dynamic of our…thing was that I didn't see your face."

"Are you having regrets?" Devon asks me, concern marring his features. "Because I don't think anything will change, Violet."

"No, I'm not having any regrets. I was just curious about how you feel." I pause momentarily. "Because I feel like it can only get better."

Devon pulls me back into him and kisses me again, groaning into my mouth. The chef tuts loudly from behind us and stomps back into the diner.

"If it's any consolation, I also think that it can only get better," Devon replies.

We lose track of time and when we finally make it back to the table, some people have already left. Freya is laughing at something on her phone with Kas and Micah.

"Oh my god, you guys totally ruined some of my pictures. Devon, why are you pretending to choke Kas in the back of this one?" Freya shows Devon the photo as he sits down. He throws his head back in unrestrained laughter.

As he laughs, I can't help but stare at his face. I only look away when Freya shoves her phone in front of me so I can look at the photos. Freya and I are smiling, our cheeks touching. In the back, you can see Kas looking pissed off with his arms crossed and Devon with two hands around his neck in a comedic choke.

Devon was behind me in those pictures the whole time?

My cheeks hurt with how wide I'm smiling. By the end of the brunch, I don't think that smile has left my face. When it's time to say our goodbyes, Devon walks me to my car and opens the door for me.

"I don't want to say goodbye," he says, watching as I settle into the driver's seat.

"I'll see you soon, right?" I ask, unsure of what to do now. I'm sure it's self-explanatory that we'll see each other soon.

"Oh yeah, that reminds me," he starts. I look up at him, shielding my eyes from the sun. "Violet, can I get your number?"

"I thought you'd never ask." I laugh, heat filling my cheeks. "Please, take my number." I punch my number into his phone, and he rings me so I also have his. He then jumps into a glossy, black car and gives me a goofy wave which earns an eye roll from Kas.

Once they're gone, I lean my head back against the car headrest and let the sun's rays warm my face as I smile to myself.

It's almost like a thick veil of uncertainty has finally been lifted, a reassurance that Devon and I are on the same page. I could reflect on insightful teachings about the value of personality over looks, but what truly stands out to me is Devon's unwavering commitment to keeping his identity obscured for the sake of fun.

A premise so stupid that at this point, it's more amusing than anything else.

Devon: On my way!
Me: Yay

I stare at Devon's message as if I haven't heard from him in years. It's only been seven hours.

"Why are you just smiling at your phone? You haven't scrolled for like thirty seconds." Ash looks at me from his usual spot on the couch, his own phone playing some obnoxiously loud music on repeat.

"Just someone I like," I say.

"A boy?"

"Yes, a boy."

Despite Ash being much younger than me, he gets very protective when it comes to me dating. Probably because he despised my ex, who in his words—and much to his own amusement considering my artistic nature—was 'more boring than watching my own paintings dry'.

"Is this the friend who rides the bike? You like him? I'd like to meet him, make sure he's good enough for you," Ash says, straightening from his slouched position.

"You probably will meet him, I think you'd get on well." I'm already telling Ash that he'll meet Devon and catch myself off guard with my confidence about Devon sticking around long enough to meet my family. Ash tries prying more questions out of me about my love life until we both hear Devon's bike an hour later.

"Don't—" I start, watching Ash get up from the sofa and sprint out of the house. I put on my shoes as fast as I can and follow him.

"What business do you have with my sister?" I hear him ask, his arms crossed over his chest. Devon takes off his helmet and mask which causes me to suck in an audible breath.

"Ash," I warn, walking across the front yard.

"You her brother?" Devon asks, smirking over at me.

"Yeah, Ashton Lee." Ash makes his voice a little lower than it usually is. I hide a giggle that works its way up my throat when I watch them shake hands. Devon looks at me with amusement, his tall frame completely swamping my brother's much smaller stature.

"Nice to meet you Ashton Lee, I'm Devon Blackstone," he

drawls. I don't think Ash hears him because he's already distracted by Devon's bike.

"Woah, cool," Ash breathes. "I seriously can't believe my goody-two-shoes sister rides on the back of this."

"Hey!" I shout as I near both of them. "I'm not a goody-two-shoes." They both gaze at me unbelievingly with an expression that says, 'whatever helps you sleep at night'.

As my brother rubs his hand over the bike's glossy exterior, his eagerness to ride it himself becomes apparent to me. Then, a question I could see him asking from miles away finally escapes his lips, "Can I ride?"

Ash and I raise our gazes to Devon. My brother's eyes are silently pleading, while I cast a glowering stare, silently urging Devon to choose his answer carefully.

"When you're older, sure. Violet tells me that you like skateboarding, so maybe you can do that for now."

"Do you skateboard?" Ash asks as if this is the defining question of the century.

"Yeah, used to do it a lot when I was your age." Ash beams and starts walking back to the house. Interrogation over. I really hope that my brother doesn't become a cop.

"Have fun Violet, I like this guy!" he calls, slamming the front door shut.

"I'm pretty sure he was meant to judge if you were safe and potentially scare you off," I say, placing the word 'safe' in an air quote.

"He did a pretty bad job of it." Devon chuckles, passing

me a backpack and placing a helmet on my head.

"He thinks you're cool, so that's probably enough for him. Where are we going anyway?" I drum my fingers on Devon's shoulders as I sit behind him on the bike.

"I'm glad you're more eager in person than texting." His shoulders hunch forward, and he pretends to silently sob.

"What do you mean?! I was so excited to see your message," I argue, swatting his back.

"You responded with 'yay'. No smiley face, just 'yay'. Jeez, it's like you hate me." Devon turns to face me with his visor up, eyes crinkling at the corners.

I shove him playfully. "You are so dramatic! Now, can you please tell me where we're going? I'm so excited." He bumps helmets with me, as if to substitute an affectionate peck on the cheek.

"I'm taking you on a date. A proper date." Butterflies flutter in my lower stomach and I rest my head on his back whilst we ride for a while. Compared to the last time I was on his bike, I don't look away from the road the entire time. I only squeal a little when Devon takes a sharp turn down a recognizable dirt path.

"Isn't this where the cops chased us?" I ask, memories of the events that transpired here come flooding back to me.

"Yeah, but there's a surprise at the end of the path." We ride through the sparse trees and enter a large open area at the edge of a cliff that reveals a beautiful view of a valley below.

The engine stops, and the rustling trees along with Devon's

thudding steps are the only things heard across the forest. He takes the backpack from my shoulders and lays out a picnic blanket a short distance from the bike.

"Our first official date with no mask, this is monumental," I state, finally managing to unbuckle the helmet. He pats the blanket next to him and I sit down. His outstretched legs cover most of the material.

"I look even better, right? Try not to jump my bones." He smiles as I watch him pull out a familiar food box, taking off the lid to reveal my favorite golden pastry.

"Baklava, of course. Where do you get this from anyway?"

"Can't tell you, I have a dealer," he says, pretending to zip his lips.

"Seriously?" Devon ignores me and holds out a piece of the sweet dessert on the end of a fork, placing it into my mouth. I don't moan this time. Devon notices because he lets out a low chuckle as I silently chew.

The view of the cliff with the sun setting behind it casts a warm glow over us. It somehow makes the dessert taste better than it did in the gas station.

"You do know that it's not just your moans that turn me on. Not moaning would never stop me from wanting to completely devour you." I struggle to swallow the Baklava after hearing Devon's words, and I look into his heated gaze.

"I know." I jump when the birds swooping and soaring in the sky over the valley squawk loudly, interrupting our otherwise peaceful picnic.

"Good, because as soon as you've finished eating, I'm going to completely ravage you," he whispers.

"Here?" I ask mid-chew.

"Don't ask stupid questions, Sweetness," he warns. "We've done it in this forest before, and I'm more than happy to do it here again." I've never eaten something so fast in my life because, true to his word, he ravages me. And just like the Baklava, it's even better than before.

Chapter 12

Violet

Mari has changed my life in the best way possible.

Allowing me access to an art studio has been amazing. I'm able to use it when it's closed for teaching, like today. It's my day off, and I'm painting here whilst I wait to pick up my brother.

Devon and I have been texting non-stop with cute, flowery messages alongside some not-so-cute pictures of various body parts. Since seeing Devon's face, I don't think the smile on my own has wavered.

Unfortunately, my mind is acting similar to that of a high schooler with their first love—distracted. I haven't been able to get my ideas straight. After dipping one of my new paintbrushes into paint, I realize that for the first time in a while, I'm stumped for ideas.

As if on cue, my phone buzzes next to me and my heart jumps when I see that it's Devon.

Devon: Where you at?
Me: Art studio
Devon: Send your location
Devon: Wanna see you

I send him my location and wait for his arrival, spending the next thirty minutes trying to conjure inspiration on what to paint. Eventually, I start to sketch a giant version of the self-portrait I did at the gas station of myself in Devon's bike helmet. After a few minutes, I hear his bike. Though, as another ten minutes pass, I realize the bike may not have been Devon's because there's still no sign of him.

I look at the doors and do a double take when I see him sitting on the chair that's holding them open. The sun hits his back, casting a glow around his muscular frame. Sometimes, I wish I could learn a different medium like sculpting so I could replicate his body and have it displayed in my bedroom or something. Maybe I should try it.

As he rises, my eyes remain fixed on him. I observe his leisurely stroll toward me until he finally crouches beside the edge of the canvas where I'm kneeling.

"How long were you sitting there?" I ask.

He leans over me and grabs one of the new paintbrushes, assessing the smooth wooden handle. He chooses the largest one that I sometimes use for murals.

"Not long enough to admire you as much as I would've liked. I love watching you paint."

"Well feel free to watch me struggle to feel inspired for the rest of the day," I sigh, tilting my head as if looking at the canvas at a different angle will spring me some more creative inspiration.

"You'll come up with ideas, I'm sure," he says, planting a chaste kiss on the crown of my head.

"I know. I think I'm just burnt out or distracted."

"You need a live model?" I look at him in mock distaste, curling my lip. I love reacting like his words are out of pocket, as if I haven't been thinking the same thing. His cheeky grin tells me that he knows I'm not as disgusted as I show.

"Alright, alright. Look, I came to take you out. Consider it a break," he tells me. The rhythmic thumping of his boots trace a circular path around the giant canvas as he fixates on it, trying to figure out what I'm drawing. Devon constantly shows interest in my work. There's something heartwarming about him caring about the things I love.

"I drew this in my little sketchpad at the gas station after our first meeting." I point toward the reference sketch next to me. "I'm just recycling my ideas."

"You wanted me so bad." He smirks and I roll my eyes at him. "But seriously, let's go somewhere. You haven't stopped doing art stuff all day."

"Well, what did you have in mind?" I ask, standing up and stretching. Devon circles behind me, guiding my arms so that they're wrapped around my chest with my elbows pointing forward.

"I don't know. Now that you don't have the thrill of talking to a faceless stranger anymore, what's something you've always wanted to do?" he asks from behind me, placing me in a bear hug and lifting me up. He squeezes me gently until my body cracks—instant relief.

"Oh my god," I moan. "I love when you crack my back for me. What are you? A chiropractor?" His eyes sparkle with playfulness and a hint of satisfaction. He looks way too proud of himself.

"So? What did you want to do?" he asks, reminding me that I never answered his previous question. I ponder on it for a few seconds with nothing in particular coming to mind. There's nothing crazy that I've wanted to do, however, I have considered getting a tattoo before.

"A tattoo," I say honestly. "I don't have one." He nods and leads me to the door of the art studio.

"Woah, let me think about it for a little bit." I pull back on his arm, though it does little to stop him from moving.

"Okay." He steps toward me and stands unspeaking for about ten seconds. His hands are perched on his belted hips, and he taps his large boot impatiently against the ground. "Okay, let's go," he rushes out, taking my arm and dragging me out of the studio.

"Devon!"

"Don't think, just do," he urges. Of course, if there was one person to encourage me to get a tattoo, it would be Devon. Or maybe Freya…or Ash.

"That is terrible advice, Devon," I stress, letting him lead me to his bike. I pat my pocket to make sure I have the studio keys, and then move the chair away so the door slams shut. "Plus, this was meant to be a break from my art, now I'm just thinking of more permanent art."

"It's a creative break," he says, kissing my neck and placing a helmet on my head. He drives us a short way to a nearby tattoo studio. The tattooists have some availability, so I fill out a form for health conditions whilst Devon flicks through a book of flash designs.

I decide on a Violet flower that I've drawn myself. It's small and delicate, tasteful for my first tattoo. I've decided on adding a touch of color to give it a nice watercolor effect. Devon watches me from his position against the wall as the tattoo artist places the template just above my ankle.

"I'm gonna get a drink, you good if I come back in a few?" Devon asks, his eyes firmly focused on where the tattooist is holding my leg.

"Sure," I say. The artist hasn't even started on mine yet because I'm too busy trying to get the perfect placement. Devon scowls at the tattooist's hand, his jaw clenching slightly when he leaves the room. I think Devon assumes that his jealous streak doesn't show that often. It does, and it's amusing every time it comes to the surface.

After a few more adjustments, the low hum of the tattoo gun begins. Devon hasn't returned by the time the tattooist finishes and wraps up my ankle. I know Devon would never bail on me, but I'm freaking out a little until I exit the room. He's sitting in the waiting room, sipping some water.

He looks a little pale, to be honest.

"All done," I say, flashing my ankle. Though, you can't really see the design under the wrap. "Are you okay? You look a bit unwell."

"I'm all good, just feeling a little dehydrated," he says, showing me the bottle of water. He cracks his neck and gives his cheek a light slap. "Did it hurt?" I shake my head, reaching for the water.

"A little...the coloring part hurt. I don't know if I'll get more though," I reply, taking a big sip.

"What? You're not going to get my name plastered across your forehead?" One of the tattooists near us chuckles at his suggestion.

"Can you imagine? That'd be crazy, tattoos are so permanent."

"They are very permanent," he muses as we pay. Devon's gaze lingers on me briefly as soon as we step out of the building, then he steals my breath with an enthusiastic kiss. I moan in surprise and pull back, looking at him in confusion.

"What was that for?" I breathe.

"The guy doing your tattoo was checking you out way too

much," he says, his voice low with annoyance.

"He was doing his job." I playfully smack Devon's chest and he shrugs.

"His job is to tattoo, not stare at my girl with goo-goo eyes whilst I'm in the room." Heat fills my body at his possessiveness, and I can't ignore that he called me his girl.

"*Your* girl?"

"Always have been, Sweetness," he says as we walk up to his bike. *Always have been.* It reminds me of the nickname he gave me, which he's been calling me since the second time we spoke.

"Devon, why do you call me *Sweetness*?"

"Because you were sweet from day one and everything about you is sweet. Your lips, your personality, your…" His eyes trail down my body, tongue pushed against the inside of his cheek. I can't help the laughter that ensues as his eyes stop at my crotch and he motions toward it with his head.

"You called me it the second time we met, though." His green eyes watch me adoringly.

"Sweet from day…two?" I smile up at him, my eyes searching his face for any trace of a lie. "If you keep looking at me like that, I'll taste how sweet you are as soon as we get back to the studio."

"That's exactly what I want, Devon," I admit. His nose flares, and he drags his hand over his face. In his impatience, he passes me a helmet so fast that it almost falls out of my hands. Then, we ride back to the studio at a speed that must be illegal. I'm surprised we don't get pulled over on the way.

As soon as we arrive, he ambushes me. Rough hands rush to take off my pants, and he pushes gently on my shoulders, forcing me to lie on the ground.

The sound of a paintbrush being tapped against a pot has me lifting my head up, only to find Devon holding one whilst pushing my shirt up.

"Should I be concerned?" I call up to him. He moves so swiftly; I barely register him on top of me as he pins me down by my thighs with his upper body sitting tall. He dips the brush into a pot of water and drags it down the side of my face.

"Don't be concerned, I'm only thinking about how much I want to see you break apart around this brush." My eyes flicker between Devon's face and the large, rounded handle of the brush that looks small in this grip. "You look scared. You're familiar with these, no?"

"Not like this," I whisper as he submerges the tip of the bristles into a can of white paint. He trails the brush over my bare torso, running it between my breasts, to my navel, circling my belly button. I release a strained breath when the cold studio air hits the wet liquid and causes goosebumps to pebble across my flesh.

"Cold?" he asks, dragging the tip of his finger over my hardened nipple. He brings his lips around one and sucks, the warmth of his mouth a nice contrast to the chilled paint.

My body writhes in response to his ministrations;

brushing, sucking, and caressing me until I'm nothing but a moaning heap.

The brush leaves my skin, but the bristles leave ghostly touches all over my flesh. Like the weight of his body, which disappears when he stands up.

"Fuck, Violet. Get up here." I pry my eyes open to see Devon sitting on a chair with a different, unused paintbrush in his hands. His eyes bore into me like hot coals as I move the short distance to him.

After placing the brush between his teeth, he uses both hands to grip my waist and lift me so I'm straddled on his lap. He cups his hand under my mouth like one would do when asking a dog to surrender something that it's not meant to eat.

"Spit," he murmurs softly. *Oh. Wait…spit?*

I hesitate. Devon raises his eyebrows impatiently, eyes firm. I spit into his palm, then watch him lubricate the paintbrush handle with my saliva. With my legs spread across his lap, he rubs the smooth, wooden end of it over my clit.

"Look at how turned on you are, Violet. You're so fucking dirty," he says, his words carrying a mocking tone. Then, he gives me his final command, "Sit on it."

Fuck. Me.

I slowly sink myself onto it with little resistance. Devon gently moves it in and out of me. "Good girl. Pretend it's my cock inside of you." I move up and down, resting my hands on Devon's shoulders for stability.

"Touch yourself, rub your clit. I know it's aching to be touched," he mumbles into my ear. I move my hand in between us as if possessed and rub my fingers over my sensitive bundle of nerves.

The friction on my clit paired with the brush has me resting my head on Devon's shoulder. The pleasure is too much, and it causes the hand on my pussy to falter lazily.

"Devon, I'm gonna cum," I whine into his neck. The heady fragrance of his cologne overwhelms my senses. He doesn't speed up the movement of the paintbrush inside of me, which makes my stomach tense up at the slow build of my release.

"You wanna cum, Sweetness?" I nod violently, sweat prickling at the back of my neck. "Too bad." He pulls out the paintbrush roughly and taps the handle on my clit.

"No," I breathe out shakily.

I ache so bad that all I can do is tremble on his lap. I *need* my release. I'm still panting as I claw at Devon's clothes, desperately trying to get to his cock.

"Taste it," he rasps, and I fumble wildly at his zipper in my attempt at trying to undo him faster. He tuts gently and I peer up at him, his tongue poking out to moisten his lower lip. "Not that, this."

Devon envelops his hand around my throat, his rough palm pressing tenderly against the front of my neck. He skims the handle of the paintbrush against my lips, and I open my mouth to taste myself on the brush.

His patience must have worn thin because in one quick movement, he lifts his hips, unzips himself, and pushes his pants down. I look at his hardened dick, the tip glistening with pre-cum. I itch to taste it, but his denial of my orgasm has me wanting it inside of me more than anything right now.

He places his hand in front of my mouth again. I understand what he wants this time because I spit and he lubricates himself. With his unwavering strength, he lifts me up with minimal effort so that his cock is teasing at my entrance. When he lowers me onto him, both of us let out a synchronized breath of relief.

After a moment, he pumps his hips up to find a rhythm and then pounds into me. I grip the back of his neck and look down at where we are joined. The sight of him sliding in and out of me is so erotic that I let out a whimpering noise from the back of my throat.

Devon pulls me into his hard torso in an all-encasing hug and fucks me harder, groaning into my ear. With his thick arms wrapped around me, I feel the handle of the paintbrush over my asshole. I tense up for a moment, then my initial shock transforms into bliss as the firm handle rubbing over me adds to my enjoyment.

"Do it," I whisper, shivering at the light sensation of it caressing my hole. He lets out a growl and pushes in the handle, testing it inside of me. He doesn't insert the entire thing, but enough so that it isn't painful—just light pressure.

I rest my head on his muscular shoulder again and clench around his dick. With both the handle of the paintbrush and his cock inside of me working in tandem, I use my hand to stimulate my clit again.

The overstimulation from everything combined draws my orgasm out of me. I flop into him, finally reaching the release that was robbed from me earlier.

Devon yanks the paintbrush out of me and throws it somewhere to his side because I hear it clatter against the ground. He hoists me up and carries me to an empty workstation. My back barely touches the surface before he continues thrusting into me, this time delving deeper inside.

"Look at me," he grunts and I struggle to follow his command, my eyes drifting closed with the euphoric feeling of his movements. "I said look at me." He grips my chin and places his forehead on mine. His hold causes my lips to press together as I fight to keep my eyes from closing.

I worm my hands under his tee, scraping my nails over his torso to feel beads of sweat drip between the defined muscle on his stomach.

"You feel so good. I will never get tired of the way your pussy wraps around me," Devon hums. "I will never get tired of you."

My dwindling orgasm returns at full force and my pussy milks him for everything he's got. He stills, roaring loudly into my neck as he reaches his release too.

His breathing is hoarse and after a few seconds, I'm convinced that I hear a deep whimper as he pulls his cock out of me. I observe him curiously when he bends down so his eyes are level with my pussy.

"Watching my cum leak out of you is one of the hottest things I've ever fucking seen." *Christ*. This man will be the absolute death of me.

"Thank god I'm on the pill." I laugh, becoming more self-conscious as he continues to stare.

I kick my foot out at him and he catches my ankle. With a gentle yank, he drags me to the edge of the table and plants a light kiss on my lips, chuckling as he steps away from me. He looks down at my half-naked body like I'm his own piece of art.

"You feeling inspired yet?" he asks.

"If I say no, could we go for round two?" He dips his head as he laughs and shakes it as if to realign his thoughts.

"For every twenty minutes you spend painting, I will make you cum." I raise one of my eyebrows.

"You drive a hard bargain, Devon," I say, trying to ignore the uncomfortable feel of drying paint on my skin.

"Yeah…hard," he jokes and I scrunch my face in disgust at his innuendo, feigning innocence as if I didn't just ask to have sex for inspiration. Devon shrugs like he's said something completely innocent too. "I came here to give you a break with your art, but we can't spend more than five minutes in a room without jumping each other."

"That wasn't a break, that was a workout." I jump off the worktop and snatch a wad of tissue out of Devon's hand.

I waddle to the bathroom to clean up, thankful that nobody else is here today. When I return, I see Devon holding a paintbrush. It's the same one that was inside of me.

"Keepsake," he says, noticing me watch him as he pockets it. I let out an unbelieving laugh.

"Weirdo."

He looks at me coyly, securing his hands behind his back. "You know, I've been feeling a little left out watching you paint ever since I helped you do that mural."

"Would you feel better if I gave you a cute little canvas to draw on next to me?" I coo as if speaking to a child.

"Yes actually, I would love that." My smile widens and Devon smiles back at me, pulling out the paintbrush from his pocket. "I've already got my brush."

Epilogue
Violet - 3 Months Later

I take another deep breath, unable to quell my nerves for my first art exhibition. This town is so small that a few members of the community recognized my contributions to the old gas station.

Now, it has its own section in the town's new museum exhibition for public art.

Tonight is the opening night, and I'm standing with my parents who are back from their flight. Devon, having already met them, stands next to me engaged in a conversation with my brother. They both get on extremely well, of course.

"Oh, I remember you drawing on the kitchen wall years ago and now look," Mom says, dabbing her eye with the sleeve of her blouse. My dad rubs her shoulder affectionately which prompts Ash to take out his phone and play a game on it.

"Several times," Dad adds. I pat Mom's back as we walk through the exhibit. The large space is filled with images of murals and graffiti along with the echoing hums of people appreciating the art.

My parents bump into another familiar face and engage in what will probably be another hour-long conversation. Ash obviously notices and lets out a loud sigh.

"Great," he mutters, eyeing up the exit door next to him. Out of the corner of my eye, Devon uses his suited body to cover Ash who manages to slip outside undetected by everyone but me.

"I saw that," I say as Devon and I break away from my parents to look at a huge picture of my mural. There's a whole corner of the gallery designated to showcase pictures of my gas station art.

"Oops," Devon replies, snatching a canapé off a tray held by one of the patrons. He notices Kas strolling up to us holding three glasses of champagne and gives him a swift nod.

"Hey guys, is this yours Violet?" Kas asks, gesturing to the mural with his full hands. Since being with Devon, Kas has opened up a lot more since he dismissed me in a state of panic at Micah's party. I'm always hanging out at their place, mostly for Devon, but also for Kas' cooking. We've even started calling their place a B&B—instead of Bed and

Breakfast, it's Baklava and Breakfast.

"Yeah, everything on this back wall is mine," I explain. Devon takes two glasses out of Kas' hands, allowing him to peruse the rest of the wall. The glass wobbles when Devon passes one to me and I gasp, thinking it might fall.

"Careful, Violet. I wouldn't want to be the cause of another spilled drink on you again," he says, flashing me a grin. I squint at him in confusion. *Again? What is he talking about?* "Micah's party...your jeans," Devon adds.

That's when it hits me. Devon was the person who knocked Vince's drink at the party.

"Oh, I thought it was you!" I laugh, giving him a playful jab to his hard abdomen.

"How else could I try and stop that guy from talking to you, if not by spilling his drink?" He shrugs.

"Ha-ha. Nice tactic. Who taught you that? A five-year-old?"

"This is nice," Kas says very matter-of-factly when he returns to us, effectively interrupting our lighthearted verbal sparring. "I like cupcakes."

"I did that one!" Devon says to him, dragging his eyes away from me to excitedly point at one of the cakes in the photo of the mural. He actually did paint that on the night when he visited me at work and was freaking out over the unsafe ladder.

"Good job, man," Kas says in a tone similar to that of an uninterested parent reacting to their child's pasta art.

"Oh, isn't this just amazing," Mari breathes with admiration as she and Freya emerge from a crowd of guests to stand beside Kas. Kas peers down at Mari and then does a double take, just as Mari looks at him. She turns her body to face him, and the wooden beads in her hair clatter with the movement.

"Hey, I'm Amari, but feel free to call me Mari," she says, holding out her hand.

"Kacper, but you can call me Kas." He places his hand in hers and I don't even think he's blinked once since laying his eyes on her. Mari doesn't seem to notice because she instantly looks at me as Freya observes the two of them, a shit-eating grin plastered on her face.

"This is phenomenal," Mari gushes and pulls me in for a hug. "Congrats, Violet."

"Phenomenal," Freya murmurs quietly as she watches Kas stare unapologetically at Mari, who is completely oblivious to his gaze. Devon shakes his head and tries not to laugh at Freya's comment.

Freya then turns to face me, her smile still wide on her face. "When you said you'd add some color I never expected this masterpiece," she says, clapping her hands together. "This is all my uncle has been talking about for the past month. He's already asking if the outside can be done. I told him he should focus on getting an electrician to fix the light in the utility closet first." I let out a laugh and Devon chuckles next to me, the dark closet bringing back a few memories.

"Thanks guys, I'm so happy you could make it," I say appreciatively. Mari suddenly pulls out a gigantic camera from a bag.

"Okay guys, can I get a photo of you both?" Mari asks gently, motioning toward Devon and me. She hands her bag to Freya, whose arms now contain both her own bag and a huge camera case.

"Sure, how do you want us?" I throw up a peace sign and Mari drags my arm down, guiding me to stand closer to Devon. She shuffles back clumsily with her camera and bumps into Kas, who grabs her shoulders to steady her.

"Sorry Kas," she apologizes quickly, and Kas says nothing, keeping his hands firmly on her.

"Okay, everybody say 'congratulations Violet!'" Freya shouts, giggling from Mari's side as she continues to watch her and Kas' awkward interaction.

"Congratulations Violet!" I say, and Devon bends down to kiss me on the cheek as the camera clicks and flashes several times.

"Beautiful, guys." Mari studies the images approvingly and Kas' hands remain on her shoulders. When she steps away from him, he snaps out of whatever trance she put him in, gulps down his champagne in one go, and strides away to look at some artwork on the other side of the exhibition.

"Mari, what have you done to Kas?" Freya asks, her head shaking in disbelief. Mari purses her lips in confusion.

"What? Oh." She turns in the direction Kas walked away

in. "Did I upset him?"

"No!" Freya, Devon, and I say at the same time.

"You did the opposite of upset him," Devon reassures her and Mari nods unconvinced, immediately changing the conversation.

"Shaved hair actually suits you, Devon. I barely recognized you when I came in," she says. "You used to have it long, right?"

"Yeah, it was more comfortable under my helmet. I've been wearing it a lot more recently." Mari looks at me with amusement and then scans the crowd for more people she can take photos of.

"Big chops for the win," Freya says, running her fingers through her copper strands which have grown a decent amount over the past few months. After having a hate-filled relationship with her hair, I guess you could finally say she's happier with it now.

"I'm gonna take some more pics around the gallery. See you soon!" Mari grabs another couple and starts positioning them for the camera. Freya follows her, flashing me a supportive smile. It's the first time they've met and Mari's gentle personality paired with Freya's more outspoken ways have them getting on more than I had hoped.

"You cut your hair so you'd be more comfortable in your helmet because you had to constantly wear it around me?" I tease, nudging Devon. He wraps his arm around my waist, and I lean my head on his chest.

"Adaptation is key," Devon says. "I also have something to show you." He takes my hand and guides me out of the exhibition and down the hall into an unused room in the building. My stomach drops. I enjoy doing stuff with Devon, but at an exhibition? With family and friends outside? I don't think so.

"Devon, not here!" I hiss, yanking my hand out of his as the door closes behind me.

"You've won a public art award and we both know that you're a fan of public things in more ways than one." My face heats furiously. "But that's not why we're in this empty room." Now I'm confused.

"Then why are we in here?" I ask.

"I want to show you my tattoo, it's healed now. I got it done the day you got yours when I said I was getting a drink. I didn't want to freak you out, so I've put off showing you it for a while."

Bile works its way up my throat. I know we moved quite fast and there's no way anything huge would've taken the same amount of time as my own tattoo. If this man has a tattooed portrait of me on him, I will run for the hills.

He unbuttons his dress shirt and I see a tiny drawing on his ribs. It's a tattoo that's much smaller than my own, and it's a similar design because it's also a Violet flower. It's beautiful. It reminds me of the way that I draw them…actually, that's exactly how I draw Violets; a squiggle without my pencil leaving the paper. I have no idea how he got his hands on my work.

"How did you get—"

The clown sketch. I was practicing signatures on the back of it. He smiles at my reaction when I recognize where he got the design from.

He pulls out his wallet and slides out a folded piece of paper. When he unfolds it, it's the sketch with various renditions of my signature on the back.

"You need to think before doing things," I say, even though I feel downright giddy.

"You think too much."

"But it's so permanent."

"I know, that's the point," he says, buttoning up his dress shirt.

"Well...I mean..." I stumble over my words.

Devon rubs his hand over his head uncomfortably. "Do you hate it?"

"I don't hate it," I reply truthfully. "It's just a little extreme, I mean, we haven't even been together a year yet."

"I'm an extreme guy," he retorts. He really is, everything I've experienced with him has been extreme.

"It's caught me off guard, but I love it." I reach out to touch his hand tenderly.

Devon's smile widens and he encases my hand in his. "Nothing's changed then," he says, his voice laced with humor.

"Catching me off guard and going to the extreme? I'd be

worried if you didn't do that." It's true. I would be worried because it wouldn't be Devon at all.

I loop my arms around his neck and bring him down so that our lips meet. His arm circles my waist and I sink into our kiss completely. He playfully nips my lips when he pulls away and then runs his finger over my swollen mouth.

"As much as I want to add a museum to our list of public spots, you have guests waiting for you," he says, patting down the straying hairs on my head and smoothing my dress down for me.

When we return to the exhibition, I notice my parents still talking to the person they bumped into earlier when Ash made his great escape. I can't see Kas anywhere, but I spot Freya and Mari talking amongst themselves in front of my art.

"I'm going to go and chat with the girls," I say, pulling away from Devon.

"Alright, I'm going to catch up with Kas." Devon jerks his head toward the other side of the room where Kas stands in front of someone else's art, his eyes unusually focused on the empty champagne glass in his hand. "He looks...troubled." We split up and as soon as I approach the girls, I realize I've ended up walking in on a conversation about Devon and me.

"Party? They met at Violet's workplace," Mari says, turning to address me. "It appears Freya and I have had a miscommunication about you and Devon." Mari covers up a giggle with her hand at Freya's reaction.

"Violet! I thought you met Devon at that party," Freya hisses, her voice a silenced shout.

"Wait, does Freya know the whole story?" I ask Mari.

"What story?" Freya turns to me. Her eyes brim with eagerness, like we're withholding vital information from her.

I've mellowed out a lot since admitting this all to Mari months ago. If faced with this question back then, I would've definitely panicked. Now, Freya's obvious impatience with wanting to know the entire story is hilarious.

"You know, the fact that for the first month of meeting, Violet didn't know who Devon was until they went for brunch because he wouldn't take off his bike helmet or ski mask at the gas station," Mari explains.

"I did know who he was, I just never saw his face." Mari gives me a doubtful look paired with a subtle shake of her head.

"She has a mask kink," Mari adds.

Freya's head bounces between us before responding with an overdramatic gasp. "Are you joking?" she asks Mari, her eyes darting to me. "Is that why you and Devon were dying with laughter at the diner?"

"Listen guys, it's old news. I don't have a mask kink and Devon and I have come a very long way since those days."

As if on cue, Kas and Devon join our little conversation corner and Freya eyes up Devon, obviously itching to ask more questions. Devon notices Freya's inquisitive scowl and looks at me, confused and scared.

"Right kids, picture time!" I spin around to find my parents walking up to us with one of the gallery workers who is holding up my dad's phone horizontally, the worn leather case flapping open.

Ash appears out of nowhere, and Mom instantly drags him to her side. She's ready to position them both in front of the lens. Mari scoots closer to Kas, and I can see him physically tense up out of the corner of my eye. He totally has a thing for Mari.

Once we're all lined up, the staff member begins to back up, ensuring we're all in frame.

"I'm not beating the mask kink accusations, by the way," I whisper to Devon.

"It's hard to beat accusations when the accusation is a stone cold fact. Now, smile."

The camera flashes and just as we can even begin to think about walking away, my mother speaks, "Right..." She walks in front of us, my father one large stride behind her. "Now just you lot." She nudges her head to the side, signaling Ash to move. He scoots beside my parents and flashes a humorous pose next to them, causing us all to laugh.

We pose for the photo and I relish in the comfort I feel with Devon.

A feeling that is no longer foreign, but one of unspoken reassurance that the person I hope will stick around for a long, long time undoubtedly feels the same way about me too.

The End.

Acknowledgments

Thank you for reading my novella. I'm very new to writing and with every project I work on, I feel myself improving. I'm still trying to find my feet with all of this!

Thank you so much to everyone who showed excitement about my work, it really motivated me to keep writing and publish. Thank you to my editor, KT and my beta readers, Stevie and Kayla.

I also want to give a huge thank you to Vic who is an amazing artist. Your drawings brought my work to life and I can't thank you enough.

Also, for family and friends: If you have magically found my work, please pretend you haven't. I want to live without the knowledge that you have read my smut scenes, especially you, S.

Connect with me

You can find me on Twitter and TikTok (@jcherryxox) and Instagram (@jcherryauthor).

Printed in Great Britain
by Amazon

27534804R00116